Billionaires for Heiresses

Second chance at true love!

Heiresses to the Bishop fortune, sisters Summer and Autumn have everything money can buy—except true love!

They thought they'd found it once with tycoons Wyatt and Hunter, but their whirlwind romances ended in heartbreak.

Now their billionaire exes are back in stunning South Africa and more gorgeous than ever! Can Summer and Autumn overcome the past for a second chance at true love?

Find out in

Second Chance with Her Billionaire

Available now!

And look out for

From Heiress to Mom

Coming soon!

Dear Reader,

For me, one of the biggest challenges (and joys!) of writing romance is taking the tropes you know and love and trying to present them in a fresh new way. Which is why you're currently holding a billionaire heroine in your hands! I wanted Summer to be on equal terms with her billionaire hero, Wyatt, not only emotionally but financially, too. And though this has very little bearing on their relationship, it was the kind of exciting spin I thought you'd appreciate—I hope!

Wyatt and Summer's story was fun to write because they both find their attraction to one another so inconvenient. Since they've been married before, they're well aware that that attraction can quickly turn into flames. But the scars of before they were ever married linger, as does their broken marriage, and they have to overcome these issues to finally be happy together...

Second Chance with Her Billionaire is a summer romance filled with flirtation, sweetness, hope and healing. I hope you love it as much as I do!

Therese

Second Chance with Her Billionaire

Therese Beharrie

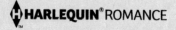

Recycling programs
for this product may
not exist in your area.

ISBN-13: 978-1-335-49928-8

Second Chance with Her Billionaire

First North American publication 2019

HARLEQUIN®
www.Harlequin.com

Printed in U.S.A.

Being an author has always been **Therese Beharrie**'s dream. But it was only when the corporate world loomed during her final year at university that she realized how soon she wanted that dream to become a reality. So she got serious about her writing, and now writes books she wants to see in the world featuring people who look like her for a living. When she's not writing, she's spending time with her husband and dogs in Cape Town, South Africa. She admits that this is a perfect life, and is grateful for it.

Books by Therese Beharrie

Harlequin Romance

Visit the Author Profile page at Harlequin.com.

Grant,
thank you for helping me believe in myself.

And to my wonderful readers,
your support pushes me into giving you the best
stories I possibly can. I appreciate you all so much.

Praise for
Therese Beharrie

"I really enjoyed this book. It had a gutsy,
sympathetic heroine, a moody hero, and the South
African setting was vividly drawn. A great debut
novel. I'll definitely be reading this author again."

—*Goodreads* on *The Tycoon's Reluctant Cinderella*

CHAPTER ONE

WHEN WYATT MONTGOMERY walked through the door, Summer Bishop took three steps forward and stopped next to the first single man she saw. The man looked over at her, smiled, and she resisted the smile that courted her own lips. He was perfect. About her height, a pleasing enough face, and he wasn't standing next to anyone else.

He turned then, offering her a glass of champagne from his tray. All desire to smile vanished. The man was a *waiter*.

Heat crawled up her neck, but she refused the embarrassment. It simply wouldn't do. Embarrassment wouldn't get her through this weekend. Though she was sure it would make an appearance, she didn't have to pay attention to it.

Not when she spoke with her ex-husband. Certainly not when she pretended a man she didn't know was her date so she could avoid said ex-husband.

Fortunately, Wyatt didn't know she'd been trying to avoid looking like a lonely loser. Yet when she felt his gaze on her, she could have sworn he did. She took a glass of champagne from the waiter's tray—why the hell not?—and downed it in one gulp. Then she returned the empty glass to the tray with a quick nod of thanks, before trying to focus on what her parents were saying.

But she couldn't.

It was as if Wyatt had issued a wordless bet the instant he walked into her parents' party. Her skin was hot, prickly, as if he knew she was desperately avoiding his gaze and was taunting her from across the room. *Look at me,* he seemed to be saying to her, *stop pretending I'm not here.* His voice was annoyingly smooth, even in her thoughts. It reminded her of all the times he'd whispered things in her ear that had—

Don't you dare, Summer Bishop.

Adhering to the voice in her head that was kindly warning her against drooling over her ex-husband's seductive prowess, she tried, again, to focus on her parents. They exchanged adoring looks. Told the family and friends who were there to celebrate their vow renewal on their thirtieth wedding anniversary about their love for one another. Their loyalty to one another.

She took a deep breath. Tried to control how the champagne now felt as if it were burning a hole in her stomach.

When that didn't work, she slipped back, behind the waiter, and then past two more people, then four, until finally she was at the glass sliding doors that led to the patio. Grass stretched out from the end of the patio to the edge of the cliff the lodge had been built on.

Whatever she felt about being forced to attend the weekend celebration for her parents' anniversary, she couldn't deny they'd picked an amazing place to have it at. Granted, it was in the small town of Wilderness, six hours away from her home of Cape Town. But the cliff overlooked the most gorgeous beach, with a path a few metres away from her leading down. It was almost worth it.

Summer walked until she could see the white-brown beach sand. It called out to her, the crash of the waves on the shore chiming in. She wished she could answer. Wished she could strip off the dress she'd chosen to wear to the celebration she wanted nothing to do with and walk into the ocean.

She settled for dragging in a full breath of the salty air.

'Daydreaming of running away?' a voice came from behind her.

The goosebumps were because of the sea breeze, Summer told herself, before straightening her shoulders and turning.

'Wyatt,' she said steadily, as if her insides didn't feel as though they were disintegrating at the sight of him. 'How pleasant to see you again.'

Those sensual lips curved into a smile that seemed decidedly feline.

'Pleasant?' he repeated, cocking his head.

She tried not to notice how the wind was mussing his hair. Or that the top button of his shirt was open, revealing tantalising brown skin that sent an irrational image of her licking it flashing through her mind.

'Not quite the word I would use,' he continued. She stared at him for a second before remembering she needed to have a sassy response.

'Okay,' she said, trying to recover when she thought there might have been a saltiness on her tongue from the skin she'd licked in her imagination, 'how about it's a surprise to see you again?'

'But it's not a surprise,' he replied quite logically, slipping his hands into the pockets of his trousers. 'We knew this was coming.'

'Unfortunately,' she muttered.

He quirked a brow, then chuckled softly to himself. 'You couldn't get out of it.'

'I—' She broke off before she could give herself away. 'I didn't try,' she lied.

Again that not quite genuine smile returned to his lips. 'I'm disappointed. I thought an occasion that would force you to see your ex-husband for the first time in two years would at least warrant an escape attempt.'

'It's my parents' thirtieth anniversary,' she said, repeating what her twin sister, Autumn, had told Summer when she'd complained about having to attend.

'It's been eight years,' Autumn had said. *'We've moved on.'*

Autumn's voice had softened, which had been the worst part for Summer. Not that she couldn't skip the weekend celebration. Not because of the reasons she wanted to escape it. It was the *sympathy*. With Autumn, when they dared speak about their family dynamics at all, it was always the sympathy.

But Summer's feelings about her family, her parents, didn't warrant sympathy. They were valid. Autumn just didn't know the entire truth of it. Eight years later, Summer still couldn't share that truth. Not with her sister, and not with the man she'd once loved.

A familiar resentment bubbled inside her.

Summer released a shaky breath and met Wyatt's eyes. She did a quick intake of air at the intensity as their gazes clashed. It felt as if that air had stumbled on its way to her lungs. Tension crackled around them; she was almost positive she felt the ground shift beneath her.

No. This wasn't a natural disaster. Rather, it was a natural effect of seeing the man she'd walked away from two years before. An after-effect, she corrected, of the passion that had resulted in a hunger that had never quite been sated between them. It didn't matter how hard they'd tried. Or how often.

'Did you try?' she asked, desperate to distract herself. 'To get out of this?'

'No,' he said simply.

Automatically, her insides twisted and turned. Reminded her of how she'd felt all throughout their short marriage.

She knew what that simple 'no' meant. It spoke of Wyatt's loyalty to Summer's father. Trevor Bishop had chosen Wyatt to be his protégé while Wyatt had still been in university. Without any reason to, Wyatt had claimed when he'd told her the story, and despite his less than stellar academic record. But Trevor had seen something in Wyatt. He'd trained that something until it had become the discipline Wyatt was now known for. Once Wyatt and Summer had started dating, Trevor had begun to nurture it.

Summer had listened to Wyatt's recollection of it when they'd started dating. Had smiled and asked questions even though it had left a bitter taste in her mouth. She should have known right then and there that there could be no future for them. Wyatt clearly idealised Trevor. But it had been too late when Summer realised Wyatt didn't only idealise him; he wanted to be like him. Wyatt wanted to be like Trevor and follow in his footsteps.

She couldn't tell Wyatt why that was a problem. Oh, she'd planned to. But she'd been caught up in the whirlwind of falling in love, and, honestly, was it so wrong that she didn't want her father to ruin that, too?

She should have let him though. Then she might

not have found herself on her honeymoon, listening to Wyatt recount his experiences with his own parents, realising once again she'd have to lie for her father.

She might have still been married, too.

Wyatt didn't believe in fate. At least he hadn't, until he'd met Trevor Bishop.

The foundation for that belief had been laid when he'd actually attended the university class Trevor had been guest lecturing at. At that point, Wyatt's attendance record had been similar to his academic record: he'd done the bare minimum to pass.

Wyatt thought about that version of himself in a very distant way. He knew it was him, but he couldn't relate to that boy any more. The boy who'd been full of hurt and anger at parents who'd abandoned him. The boy who'd had no purpose. Perhaps that was why meeting Trevor Bishop that day had been so significant. If he hadn't, that boy would have become a hurt and angry man.

That was not the man Wyatt was today.

Or so he'd thought until now, seeing his ex-wife for the first time since they'd signed their divorce papers.

Her arms were at her sides, her hands curled into fists, her expression painfully tight. All signs she didn't want to be there. Proof she'd been lying when she said she hadn't tried to get out of this event, too. She hated being there. The only reason he could think of as to why was him.

Hurt curled in his belly; anger simmered in his veins.

It made no sense then that his eyes had immediately been drawn to her when he'd arrived minutes earlier. Or that he'd followed her outside, away from the crowd of people who would have protected him from the pain, the anger.

Yet there he was, desperately pretending seeing her again didn't stir up emotions he'd rather not feel.

'Why would I try to get out of this?' he asked, his voice deliberately pleasant. She'd started it, hadn't she? 'It's an all-expenses-paid vacation to a beautiful lodge along the beach of one of South Africa's most beautiful places.'

'Oh, yes,' she replied dryly. 'I'd forgotten about your meagre wealth.' Her eyebrow lifted. 'I'd forgotten how poorly travelled you are.'

He resisted the smile, though he accepted the jibe. She was right. He didn't need anyone to pay for anything for him these days. It was a stark contrast to his childhood. To the days after his father had left and his mother had drunk herself into oblivion. When he'd had to steal his schoolmates' lunches for food or wear his father's clothes when his had grown too small.

That kid could never have imagined having the money Wyatt had today. Nor would he have imagined the trips Wyatt now took as the right-hand man of the CEO of Bishop Enterprises. He flew all over the world to secure deals for the import/export company.

His life had changed dramatically. All because fate had urged him to attend class on the day Trevor Bishop had been there.

Then again, fate had brought him Summer, too. Look how that had turned out.

'Let's put it down to the respect I have for my ex-father-in-law, then, shall we?'

'Yes,' she said after a moment. 'Let's.'

Her eyes met his, and he thought he saw a flash of vulnerability there. It quickly slipped behind a cool expression, which he was grateful for. A long time ago he'd cared about what was behind that cool expression. Hell, he'd thought he'd seen exactly what was behind that cool expression.

Because it was almost identical to the expressions he'd worn. The ones that said, *I'm pretending, but you'll never know why.* Or, *I'm hiding something, and you'll never know what.*

Back then he'd thought he knew why Summer was pretending. What she was hiding. She was the strong and powerful heiress of the Bishop empire; she had to act that way. She was hiding that she didn't want to.

Except now he wasn't so sure he'd known anything about her after all. Or was he just sour that she knew enough about him to think he wasn't worth the woman behind the mask any more?

Whatever it was, when she deemed him worthy to see the real her, it made him lose his ability to reason. He'd proposed spontaneously; married her within weeks of that proposal.

He should have signed the divorce papers at the same time and saved himself some trouble.

'Where is Autumn?' he asked, trying to get his mind off the memories. 'I thought she'd be here.'

Not that he noticed anyone after he saw Summer.

'She will be.' Summer clenched her jaw, then relaxed it. Forcibly, he thought. 'She's putting the final touches on a cake for a wedding tomorrow. Then she'll have to get it to the actual wedding, so she'll only be here on Sunday. Conveniently,' she added, distinctly softer than her other words.

For some reason, it amused him.

'Pity.'

'It is.' She narrowed her eyes.

'What?'

'You're using that dry tone that tells me you're making fun of me.'

'I'd *never* make fun of you.'

'You did it again.'

'Summer, I'm not responsible for the way you interpret my tone.'

He smiled easily at her, mostly because he knew she'd find it irritating. He really missed irritating her.

'As obstinate as ever, I see.'

'As sensitive as ever, *I* see.'

'I am not—' Summer broke off when his smile widened. 'I should have tried harder to get out of this.'

'Yes,' he agreed, not acknowledging her confirmation that she had tried to skip the event. 'It would have saved you a lot of trouble.'

Her expression went blank, her eyes shifting to the doors of the dining hall they'd come out of before resting on him again.

'Did you come out here specifically to annoy me, Wyatt?'

Since he couldn't tell her the real reasons he'd followed her—he didn't fully know what they were—Wyatt said, 'I did. I'm happy to see I'm succeeding.'

She shook her head and looked up, and for the first time he noticed her hair wasn't loose. Usually, she wore her curls wild and free; today, her hair was tied back into a stern bun. Sleek, sure, but tamed to within an inch of its life. It bothered him.

Or maybe what bothered him was the hunger that was restless in his body. As if his cells had been starved and were now being offered a feast. Which was, he supposed, not untrue. For two years, his eyes had been starved of the beauty of her face. He couldn't blame them for wanting to sate their hunger, despite the anger; despite the hurt.

So he allowed them to sweep over the oval slope

of her brown eyes; the curve of her cheekbones; the dusting of freckles on the skin of her cheeks. He let them check whether the slight scar at her temple was still there, and if her lips were still pink and full and perfect for kissing.

He stopped himself then, because thinking about kissing and Summer at the same time was taking it too far. The prickling of his body told him so, as did the way those pink, full lips of hers parted. Which made him realise his eyes had dropped to her lips and had stayed there. That he was now showing her his hunger; revealing to her his feasting.

Though he warned himself not to, his eyes lifted to hers, and their gazes locked. A stampede could have passed them, the animals hurling themselves off the edge of the cliff, and he wouldn't have noticed. He would have just kept looking into Summer's eyes. He would have kept trying to see if his tainted past had been worth sacrificing that pull between them, especially when it still seemed to be alive and kicking.

He stepped back at the unexpected thought. When he realised it took him closer to the cliff, he took a step to the side. In his current state, being close to anything that might put him at risk of falling wasn't a good idea.

So run away from Summer, then, a voice in his head told him.

He swallowed.

CHAPTER TWO

SUMMER'S LEGS HAD gone unsteady under her. She desperately wanted to walk away from Wyatt; she couldn't. Because she was worried her legs wouldn't carry her away, yes, but also because it was more than just her legs that were unsteady.

It was her mind. It was offering her memories of that short period when they'd been happy together. When his snark had attracted her almost as much as it had annoyed her. When she'd been able to enjoy the breadth of his shoulders, the short curls of his hair, his unreasonably handsome face.

Her heart was unsteady, too. It was complaining about being put under this much pressure, torn between being happy to see him and aching at what seeing him reminded her of.

Heartache. Loss. Failure.

Loneliness.

She resented the feelings almost as much as she resented Wyatt's admiration for her father. She still didn't know how he could admire the man who'd broken his family with his infidelity. Who'd broken her heart by telling her to keep it a secret from her sister and mother…

Because Wyatt doesn't know.

Oh, yes. That was how.

'I should get back,' he said.

She nodded. 'Me, too.'

They both turned, and their shoulders touched. Her head turned so sharply for her to glare at the offending part of her body she was afraid she'd damaged her neck. But she didn't spend much time thinking about it. She was too busy looking at her traitorous shoulder.

How had they got so close they could touch like this anyway?

Not liking that she hadn't noticed it, she took a deliberate step to the side at the same time he did. Her head lifted from her shoulder to his face; she narrowed her eyes. It was fine that she didn't want to touch him, but how dared he not want to touch her? It didn't matter what his reasons were—and she refused to think about her own—it was offensive.

'You can't kill me with a glare,' he told her calmly, as if he were completely unaware of what had happened.

'Doesn't mean I can't try,' she replied sweetly, walking ahead of him before he could respond.

Except that the move wasn't quite as impactful as she'd hoped it would be. Her heels sank into the grass. Because she'd been storming off—quite appropriately—she hadn't been prepared to get stuck. Momentum pushed her forward and for the longest seconds of her life, Summer thought she was going to fall on her face. In front of her ex-husband. And a bunch of her parents' wealthy friends she didn't think much of.

Which didn't mean she wanted them to see her fall.

Instead of falling, though, she was pulled back up against a hard body. Her mind needed a moment to recover, so it took longer than she would have liked to realise the body was behind her, not in front. It took even longer to realise that she recognised the feel of that body against her.

No, no, no, no, no.

Wyatt had *not* saved her from falling. He was *not* standing behind her, his hard, delicious body pressed against hers, his arm around her.

She was not remembering how many times he'd seduced her from this very position. Sliding an arm around her waist, pulling her against him, dipping his head to the nape of her neck, brushing his lips over the sensitive spot he knew was there.

She was not thinking about how she would lean her head back to give him better access. Or how she'd let out a sound that had been somewhere between a purr and a moan when he obliged her. When he'd started seducing her more earnestly, his hand would move from her waist over her breast, linger there while teasing the sensitive spot in her neck. She'd push back onto his—

Two seconds later she'd stepped out of her shoes and was facing him.

'Thank you,' she said, her face burning. She couldn't command the embarrassment back now, though a part of her tried. She hoped he'd think it was because of her almost-fall rather than her overactive imagination.

He studied her for a moment, his expression unreadable, before bending down and removing her shoes from the ground. He placed them in front of her, looking up at her expectantly. She blinked. Then realised he wanted her to step back into them and felt the faint call of hysteria.

That was what this intense desire to laugh was, wasn't it? And did he really think she wanted to touch him again after what her mind had put her through minutes before?

Oh, wait, she thought. He didn't know what she was thinking. She also couldn't keep acting like a lovestruck teenager. She was feeling attraction. She was attracted to him. Had been the moment she'd seen him at her father's Christmas party three years before; would still be now, two years after their divorce. Attraction didn't simply go away because they were no longer together. In fact, it had probably grown because she knew what it was like to be with him.

Yes, that was the perfectly logical explanation for why she was so overwhelmed by how sexy he was. Simple, biological attraction.

She took a breath and slid one foot into her shoe. When she was unable to think of a way to avoid it, she rested her hand on his shoulder and stepped into her other shoe. He waited to see if she was steady, then rose. Slowly, languidly, as if giving her a chance to grow accustomed to his new position.

He was still much taller than her; his shoulders broad, his torso and hips narrow, held up by powerful legs.

And suddenly simple biological attraction didn't seem like the truth.

He lowered his head, meeting her eyes lazily.

'Put your weight on the balls of your feet,' he told her, before walking away.

She didn't walk after him. Instead, she took a moment to regroup. She had known this would be hard. She had known seeing him would be hard.

Seeing him at a celebration for an occasion she didn't quite believe in? Hard. Seeing him around her father? Hard.

But she hadn't expected this. This attraction that awoke every part of her body. Or the sharp quips or any discussion, really. She'd thought she'd avoid him. Avoidance was the perfect solution to any problem, she found.

Up until the moment when she was forced to face what she was avoiding.

Like how steady her parents were even though her father had had an affair; and how unsteady she still felt because of it. She was still an outsider to her family. To their unit: her mother, her father, Autumn. She'd been outside that unit for years. But she hadn't put herself there.

She couldn't tell her mother or Autumn that. Not when they'd moved on and their family had recovered from her father's affair. She couldn't tell Wyatt either. He looked at their family with the kind of awe that came from not having a supportive one as a child. He looked to her father as the gold standard. Of being a businessman, a husband, a father. Unfortunately, he didn't know that Trevor had put the first before the last two.

Or that he had done the same, and she'd ended up feeling like an outsider to their marriage, too.

She took a breath. Thought happy thoughts. Strangely, those thoughts were still of the times when she didn't have to pretend to be a part of her family. They'd spent summers travelling the world; had almost daily family dinners. Her father's phone had been glued to his hand the entire time, but at least he'd been there.

He'd been more involved when she'd expressed interest in the company though. She'd spent weeks following her father around the Bishop Enterprises building when she was younger. She'd looked at how Trevor had turned the business her grandfather had started into an empire, and she'd been proud. So proud she'd wanted to be a part of it.

Until she'd found out he'd cheated on her mother and it had all felt like a lie.

She shifted gears, but what was left in her bank of happy memories was of her and Wyatt. Of the dates where she'd fallen in love with his kindness, his wit. Where he'd listened to her, really listened, and she'd felt understood for the first time since… since her father had told her she couldn't speak honestly to the two people she loved most.

As she thought it, it felt as if tar had been smeared all over her happy memories. They felt icky now. Messy. Shameful. No one could blame her for avoiding things when thinking about them turned out like this.

Not that she'd care if they did. Her plan was to stay on the outskirts of her parents' celebrations as far as she could anyway. She'd wait until Autumn arrived and use her sister as a shield. Against Wyatt, too, she thought, reminding herself to stay away from him.

She turned then, putting her weight on the balls of her feet as instructed, and walked towards the patio. As soon as she got there, her parents' guests started walking through the doors. She quickly stepped aside, keeping out of the way as she took in the scene.

The guests had blankets and picnic baskets, and were walking onto the grass in groups. Some of them nodded a head at her in greeting; she offered them one back. They spread out their blankets and began to relax on the grass, clearly preparing to watch the sun set.

She couldn't fault the actual activity. Watching the sunset on a cliff overlooking an ocean was pretty great. Romantic, too, which she supposed her parents had intended. The weather was warm in that careless way summer had. The waiters were moving around taking drink orders so the warmth would soon be combatted by icy cocktails and cold beers.

'The blankets and baskets are inside,' Lynette Bishop told her, stopping in front of Summer.

'Okay,' Summer replied slowly, looking past her mother to where her father stood in the doorway with Wyatt. Both their stances were casual; they were obviously comfortable with each other. Resentment pushed up in her throat, and she told herself to shake it off. Deliberately, she looked back at her mother.

'I think I'm going to go back to the cabin, Mom,' she said with forced calm. 'It's been a difficult week and—'

'I'm sure it has been,' Lynette interrupted. 'Running your own business must be so exhausting,' she continued, as if she hadn't spent her entire life running the Bishop social empire, which was pretty much its own business, 'which means you have to find time to relax.'

'I know.' She smiled. 'Like going to bed early so I can get some sleep.'

'Or taking a blanket and watching the sun set with your parents, whom you love.'

Lynette's smile was equal parts sweet, equal parts threatening. As if she were not only daring Summer to go back to the cabin, but daring Summer to contradict her statement, too.

But Summer had no desire to give in to her mother's dares. The first had been her taking a chance anyway; the second wouldn't be true. She *did* love her parents, which was why all of what they'd gone through—and what she, alone, was still going through—was so hard. Besides, she was there, after all.

She sighed. 'If I stay, I'm not sitting with you and Dad. I'd prefer not to embarrass myself like that.'

Lynette gave a light laugh. 'You will stay, but that's perfectly acceptable.' Her face changed slightly. 'Would you prefer sitting with Wyatt?'

'Mother.'

'You're not looking forward to the reconciliation?'

'I didn't look forward to it, no. Since we already had it, I can say that I was right not to.'

Her mother didn't say anything for a moment. Summer wondered whether it was because Lynette wanted to encourage her to sit with Wyatt. Her parents had always liked him. Which made sense, considering Wyatt so badly wanted them to like him.

It wasn't that Wyatt pretended around them, but rather that he wasn't entirely the man she'd fallen for when they were all together. She'd tried to avoid spending time with her parents during her marriage because of it. It hadn't helped. Wyatt had turned into that man anyway.

'Fine, dear,' her mother told her with a pat on the shoulder. 'You can sit by yourself. I just want you here with us.'

Summer nodded, swallowing her sigh. This added to her problem. Her mother was the same person she'd been before the affair. It hadn't changed her, finding out. Not for the first time, Summer wondered if that would stay the same if her mother found out Summer had known before Lynette had.

Not wanting to think about it, Summer walked past Lynette to get a blanket and basket, hesitating when she reached her father and Wyatt.

What was the protocol with this? Did she ignore them, or did she join in the conversation?

Because neither appealed to her, she offered them both a smile—small, polite, like the one she would have given to two strangers—and passed them. A hand closed around her arm before she could let out the breath she was holding.

'Are you looking for a blanket?' Wyatt asked her.

Her head lifted, though she wanted to stare at the hand that was sending uncomfortable shots of electricity through her body. Staring might make him stop touching her. She resisted, looking from her father, who was watching them with interest, back to Wyatt instead.

'Yes. I was told they're in here.'

'They were.' He lifted a hand, which held a blanket. 'This is the last one.'

There was a beat when she wondered what he expected her to say. *Okay? Thank you for telling me? Can we share?*

When all of them rang true, Summer let out a little breath.

'Okay. Thank you for telling me. Can we share?'

There was another beat, but this time it was long and awkward, making her stomach turn.

'Of course we can share, Summer,' Wyatt said slowly, *politely*, and she gave him a bland stare.

When she looked at her father now, he seemed almost amused. Which annoyed her, though she wouldn't show it.

Avoid, avoid, avoid.

'I'll leave you two to it, then,' Trevor said, giving them both a nod before walking out to join Lynette. Summer stared after him while the ball of tension in her stomach that was always there when she was around her father unravelled. She took a deep breath.

'That was weird,' Wyatt commented before she could say anything.

'What?'

'You were being weird just now.'

'I'm sorry, this is the first time I've had to interact with an ex-husband,' she said flatly.

His expression tightened, but he continued. 'I'm not talking about that. I'm talking about you and your father.'

Her heart immediately thudded in her chest, but she tried for an easy smile. 'Not sure what you mean, Montgomery.'

He blinked. She didn't need that to tell her she'd taken him by surprise though. She'd only ever called him by his surname when things had been good between them. When things had been easy. It hadn't been her intention, but she hoped it would be enough to distract him.

'I'll get us a basket,' she said, and headed to where the wait staff were standing.

She smiled at the waiter who handed her the wicker basket, then did a mental shoulder roll before heading back to Wyatt. She couldn't let him suspect anything was wrong. She'd hidden the turmoil between her and her father for the entire year she and Wyatt had been together. She hadn't let him see how his desire to be like her father had affected her either.

She wouldn't reveal it now. Which would be an effort, considering the anniversary—the vow renewal—was challenging for her.

But she would play the part. She wouldn't let Wyatt suspect she was keeping secrets. She wouldn't let her mother and Autumn suspect it either. She'd just let them all think she was being her usual surly self. And everyone could go on pretending everything was fine.

She swallowed down the wave of nausea.

When Wyatt reached out for the basket, she handed it to him, then took the blanket instead. In silence, they made their way to the grass. There was only one spot free, a little to the side of the cliff, where they wouldn't have a perfect view of the sunset. But the spot offered them a different view. Of the large green trees on the hills a short distance away; the houses amongst the trees; the ocean crashing against the rocky bases of the hills. Not seeing the sunset didn't seem so bad, considering.

She spread out the blanket in front of them, looked down. Realised she wasn't entirely sure how to sit. All her options seem to involve inelegance or flashing some poor unexpected guest.

'Need help?'

Her body tensed at the prospect of his touch, but she managed to arrange her expression into a careful smile.

'Yes, please.'

Wyatt held her hand as she settled onto the blanket, legs to the side, one angled over the other. Before he sat down, a waiter approached him with two glasses of what she thought was lemonade. She couldn't be sure since the ice filled the glass just as much as the liquid did. He handed her one of the glasses, then lowered his body onto the blanket.

'What is this?'

'Lemonade,' he confirmed. 'I ordered it when you went to fetch the basket.'

'Quick work,' she commented. 'Thanks.'

It was all either of them said for the longest time.

'How badly do you wish someone else had got the last blanket?'

'On a scale from one to ten?' she asked thinly. 'An eleven.'

'Ten being how badly you wanted it to be me then?'

She glanced over at him. His mouth curved. She let out a breath.

'You're being a lot less prickly than earlier.'

'I don't know what you're talking about.'

She didn't even blink. 'Sure you don't.'

Something flickered in his eyes. 'I thought it might be easier if I were nicer to you.'

'No, you don't,' she replied. 'You don't believe in being nice for the sake of easy.'

The edges of his mouth turned down. 'True,' he said softly. The tone of it brushed over her skin. 'Fine, then. Your father asked me to be.'

CHAPTER THREE

HE HADN'T MEANT to tell her that, and, somehow, he'd made it sound worse than it had been.

Which he knew based on the way the air around them was now standing to attention.

'Is that what you two were talking about just now?' she asked stiffly.

'Yes.'

'He asked you to be nice to me.'

It wasn't a question, and it sounded as if she was speaking to herself more than she was to him.

'Well,' Wyatt said, 'he said that he knew this was tough on the both of us. And he…suggested that it might make things easier if I cut you some slack.'

She made an impatient sound deep in her throat. 'Is that why you were being so polite earlier?'

'Yes.'

'Just because my father asked?' Her voice sounded strangled.

He shrugged. 'It made sense.'

'Because I'm the big bad wolf,' she muttered.

The anger he thought he'd set aside—much as he had the attraction—stirred. 'I think the person who asks for a divorce is generally the big bad wolf in the tale.'

'Not the person who signs the divorce papers without a fight?' she retorted, but quickly shook her head before he could reply. 'I'm sorry. I didn't mean that.'

He didn't believe her.

'I wasn't talking about you anyway,' she continued. Closed her eyes. Opened them. 'And you're right. It does make sense.' There was a pause. 'How about this view?'

He didn't reply. Was afraid if he did, they'd find themselves doing a post-mortem of their marriage. He'd decided—one desperate, torturous night two years ago—that the best thing he could do for himself was to forget that Summer Bishop existed. It had been hard to do considering the building he worked in bore her name, but he'd been determined.

For the most part, he'd succeeded. He'd buried himself in his work. Deeper, he qualified, since he hadn't stopped digging since Trevor had given him his first job opportunity. Trevor had shown him work was the kind of investment Wyatt could make without regret.

It had been the first of many lessons Trevor had taught him. Wyatt had paid attention to all of them. Who could blame him? Trevor had a life Wyatt hadn't dared to dream of when he'd been a child. Stability, security. Love, happiness. When Wyatt had realised it was possible, he'd been determined to do whatever it took to try and get it. The professional and financial success he'd managed; the personal success, not so much.

He wasn't sure why he'd thought things would be different with Summer. He'd had a string of short-lived relationships before her. A long-term relationship was bound not to work. Especially not with her.

It hadn't mattered that he'd thought she was a perfect match for him. Or that their life together had had the potential to inspire others—just as Trevor and Lynette's had inspired him. He and Summer weren't…suited. She'd made that clear when she'd asked for the divorce. When she'd said she wanted to focus on her business; that she didn't have time for their marriage.

A lie, he'd known immediately. What she hadn't had time for was him.

What else was new?

He shook the sinister question out of his head. He'd learnt his lesson. He wouldn't rise to her bait about how he hadn't fought for their marriage. She'd decided he wasn't good enough to be her husband. How was he supposed to fight that?

He did linger on her comment about her father though. It spoke to that thing he'd picked up between Summer and Trevor earlier. That…vibe. He wasn't sure how they were connected; he only knew they were.

'When people say silly things about Africa, I wish I could show them this,' she said suddenly, and he looked over. Her face had lost some of its earlier tension, making it seem softer.

Soft Summer made him think of Vulnerable Summer. Behind-the-Mask Summer. The effect of that was immediate. Potent.

He cleared his throat. 'You mean, you'd rather show them this than the picture of your pet lion?'

Her lips curved. 'Exactly. I'd prefer not to exploit Nala like that.'

Wyatt chuckled, and wondered if he should be allowing himself to enjoy her. She'd hurt him. This was the first time since he'd truly come to terms with the fact that she had—since signing the divorce papers—that he was seeing her. He shouldn't even be wondering about enjoying her. He should be tempering the anger; taming the hurt.

And yet he still found himself enjoying her.

'I'm sure Nala appreciates it.'

'I don't do it for the fame, Montgomery. It's the right thing to do.'

She lifted her glass and took a slow sip of her lemonade. His lips twitched. Heaven only knew why. He shouldn't be attracted to her sense of humour. He shouldn't be watching her tongue slip between her lips as it checked for leftover lemonade. That moment earlier should have been enough warning about his attraction to her. When he'd felt her body against his after he'd caught her, her butt pressing into an area that had immediately awakened, as if it had been in a deep slumber since her.

He'd told himself the fact that he'd had no sexual interest in anyone since his divorce was normal. He'd never been through a divorce before to know for sure, but it seemed logical. *Of course* not wanting to risk his heart in another relationship seemed logical.

Until he'd realised he'd never risked his heart in any of his relationships before Summer. He'd had a distinct sexual interest in the women he'd dated before her though.

Then he'd seen Summer again and his body had responded to her as if she were the prince in a fairy tale; he, the princess put under a spell that only she could break.

He was immediately disgusted with himself for the fanciful notion. The anger he'd been struggling to keep a grip on was suddenly firm in his hands, too. *She* was making him feel this way. Even though she'd left him as everyone else in his life had, he was allowing her to make him feel this way. Which made him just as angry at himself as he was at her.

He was angry that she made his body betray him. That for the second time that day, she'd called him by his surname. He was angry that he missed that. And that even though he'd missed it, he still didn't want her to use it.

It was something intimate. Something people

who were close to one another did. He and Summer weren't close any more; they no longer shared intimacies. She had no right to use it in the same way she had when they'd still been married.

His anger had nothing to do with the fact that no one else in his life called him that now. It had nothing to do with the hurt he felt at that fact; or the longing; or the inevitable resentment. He still had Trevor. So what if their relationship wasn't a surname-calling one? Relationships didn't only look one way. Being close to someone didn't only look one way.

This was the worst part about seeing Summer again, he thought. Contemplations on things he'd gleefully ignored most of his life. *She* did this to him. She made him think about his feelings. Sure, feelings were natural—but they were feelings, and he had no patience for them. Not when he knew he shouldn't entertain them.

Not entertaining them had got him through a father who'd left when he was ten. It had helped him survive a mother who'd almost died from alcohol poisoning when he was fourteen. It had kept him sane when he'd been bounced between his mother's house and foster care until he was eighteen. It had kept him from hitting rock bottom when he'd returned from his first term at university to find out his mother was selling the family house and was nowhere to be found.

'I can hear you stewing,' she commented into the silence that had grown tense as he'd been thinking.

'I'm not stewing.'

'You don't have to stay here, you know,' she replied, ignoring his denial. 'I do, because my mother asked me to, and, obligation.'

'You don't think your father was asking the same of me when he told me to cut you some slack?'

'No,' she said simply. 'Though if he was, you've fulfilled that obligation. You've been perfectly cordial to me.' There was a brief pause. 'I'll be sure to tell him that if you like.'

'Why does this sound like a bribe?' he asked, feeling more sullen than angry. 'I leave, you get to spend time alone and you tell your father I've been nice.'

She snorted. 'No one said anything about *nice*.' She tilted her head towards him, though her eyes were still on the view ahead of them. 'Cordial. Or polite, though they mean the same thing. That's my final offer.'

He didn't reply, but he didn't move either. He supposed that gave her an answer.

She sighed. 'So, you're going to be stubborn.'

'I'm not going to leave the first event at your parents' anniversary celebration because you asked me to.'

'Especially not if you think my father would disapprove.'

'What does that have to do with anything?'

Her eyes slid over to his, and there was a sadness there he'd seen come and go during their short relationship. His last memory of it had been outside the lawyer's office after they'd signed the divorce papers.

'Everything,' she answered softly. 'It has everything to do with it.' There was a pause. 'But if you feel like you have to stay for his sake, I won't stop you.'

'Thanks,' he answered dryly, though he was still thinking about what her answer meant.

'We don't have to talk though.' She looked out into the distance again. 'In fact, I'd prefer it if we don't. We can just pretend that we did.'

'You were the one who heard my stewing,' he muttered.

'Pretend I didn't interrupt you.'

And he did. For all of a minute.

'What did you mean by that?' he asked. '"It has everything to do with it",' he repeated, when he saw she didn't understand.

'It doesn't matter.'

'Then tell me.'

'That would cause unnecessary drama.'

'So it *does* matter.'

'Let me rephrase this,' she said, turning towards him now. He didn't think she realised it, but in that movement, she'd cut off the world around them. 'It's too late to matter.'

He frowned. 'This cryptic thing doesn't work for you, Summer.'

'I don't particularly enjoy it either.'

She shifted again, her body seemingly relaxed as she set one hand on the ground behind her. The other still held her half-full lemonade. He'd forgotten about his. He took a sip, barely tasting it.

'We're being watched,' she said, a pleasant expression on her face. 'So I'm going to drink the rest of my lemonade, order another, and check the picnic basket so it doesn't look like we're arguing.'

'We aren't,' he said, for his benefit and hers. She gave him a look, but proceeded to finish her drink.

It made sense that they were being watched. And it explained why Summer had taken on a relaxed stance when he knew she felt anything but relaxed. He followed her lead, not wanting to give anyone something to talk about. Though he knew that their presence there together would already be cause for discussion.

Summer had stopped attending Bishop events after their divorce. It had been gossiped about endlessly for months after. There was a period when Wyatt couldn't join a group of people without them falling silent; the universal sign that he'd been the topic of conversation.

It had bothered him. He knew she struggled with maintaining her Summer Bishop persona. Cool, infallible heiress. It had been the first thing that had bonded them. He'd found her crying on the steps of her parents' Christmas party; when she'd joined the party though, there'd been no sign of it.

He knew what it was like to have to pretend everything was fine when it wasn't. His mother had made sure of it when she'd told him to keep her alcoholism a secret.

If Summer wasn't attending Bishop events, it must have meant that she could no longer continue with the façade. He wouldn't have been concerned about it had he not known she'd created the façade for the sake of her family, too. To support the idea of the Bishop unit, which was part of what made them so powerful.

He hated to think he'd somehow damaged that. Her ability to pretend or her relationship with her family. When he'd summoned the courage to ask Trevor about it, Trevor had gone quiet. Then he'd said it wasn't Wyatt's fault.

Wyatt didn't quite believe that. But if it was his fault, maybe he could do something about it now…

'You know,' he started easily. He didn't want to scare her off or alert her to how much what he was about to say smarted. 'Part of the reason I'm surprised you're here is because you haven't attended a single event since the divorce.'

Her eyes flickered up to his. There was something there before her expression became unreadable. She calmly opened the basket and pulled out the bottle of champagne that had been carefully laid over clear boxes of cheeses, breads, and fresh fruits.

She popped it open, seemingly forgetting that she'd told him she would be ordering another lemonade. She poured herself a generous glass. Then she leaned back, lifting the liquid to her lips as if his question hadn't affected her in the least.

Well. He supposed he hadn't damaged the mask then.

'I didn't realise you'd noticed.'

'It wasn't subtle.'

Cool it, he warned himself when his voice took on a hard edge.

'I was tired of being subtle.'

'The mystery still doesn't suit you.'

'Luckily what suits me is none of your business.'

Their gazes locked. All the muscles in his body tightened.

The anger was there now. He didn't have to long for it, or wonder where it had gone to. But it didn't cool down the attraction that had flared the moment they looked at each other.

Oh, who was he kidding? The attraction was *always* there. Through dating and through marriage and even through divorce. And now. Now when she made him think and feel when he would rather not.

His eyes slipped from hers almost of their own accord, lifting to the severity of the hairstyle that had once been a wild, lazy afro halo around her face when they'd been together. Being tied so tightly at the nape of her neck accentuated her already prominent cheekbones. It gave her a more drastic beauty rather than the easy beauty of her other hairstyle.

His gaze lowered to her dress. It was lace, with sleeves that went just past her elbows and a skirt that ended just past her knees. Perfectly appropriate for the occasion, which he knew would be why she chose it.

It wasn't for the reason that occurred to him now: so he could enjoy the way its material skimmed the curve of her breasts, the slope of her waist, the rounding of her hips.

He could still feel the softness of her body under his fingers; could still see her brown skin stretched over it. He remembered how he would run his fingers over the arches of her body. Remembered how he would trace the stretch marks, the indents at her hips, her stomach, her butt. How he'd follow his fingers' path with his lips, how they'd—

He took a deep breath, rearranging his body so that he sat up straight, as if somehow the stern position would help him regain control of his mind. His body. His emotions. And then his eyes met hers, and he saw an answering heat there.

'Sure, Bishop,' he murmured softly. 'Let's keep telling ourselves we're none of the other's business, shall we?'

CHAPTER FOUR

SUMMER PULLED THE jersey she'd thrown on tighter around her as a light breeze floated in the air. Not because the breeze was cold. The summer's day had appropriately ended in a warm evening. But the feel of the wind against her skin felt a lot like Wyatt's gaze on her during the picnic. And the sound of it was almost exactly the tone of Wyatt's voice when he'd told her they weren't each other's business.

She was annoyed that her mind would go there, but she was also beginning to realise she'd have to accept *annoyed* as her permanent state of mind this weekend.

And *achy* as the permanent state of her body.

It was the reason she was wandering around the lodge's property in her nightshirt at ten in the evening. She'd walked around the communal pool, and had been tempted, for a second, to dip her achy body in its coolness before she'd thought about the energy that would require. She'd walked along the edge of the cliff overlooking the ocean. Now she was at the wooden bridge that connected the side of the lodge where her parents and a select few friends stayed with the other side, where the rest of the guests had their cabins.

Trees lined the entire length of the bridge on either side. One thick branch extended from the left to the right, high enough so as not to obstruct anyone's way. It gave the lodge a woodsy feel; a stark difference from the beachside atmosphere she got when she took a few steps in the direction of her cabin and saw the ocean.

'You couldn't sleep either?'

Summer didn't need to turn to recognise the voice. The gooseflesh that had once been her skin confirmed it to her. She wished now that the wind were the only thing her skin had to contend with.

She stayed where she was, but she said, 'It usually takes me a while to unwind after a long week.'

'I know.'

She felt him move closer, somewhere over her shoulder, but she refused to turn.

'No, I don't think you do,' she said. 'My days have got a lot longer since our divorce.'

'How is that possible?'

'Is that a criticism?' she forced herself to ask lightly. 'Because you know I was only taking my cue from you. Working hard. Focusing on building a name for myself.'

'You didn't have to.'

She turned around. 'I didn't have to what? Work hard? Or build a name for myself?'

'You didn't have to start your own business,

Summer,' he said, his expression smooth as stone. 'You didn't have to work as hard as I did. You already had a place at Bishop Enterprises. I had to earn mine.'

She clenched her jaw. Her father had been busy since her and Wyatt's divorce. Though telling Wyatt she'd once had plans to work in the family business was tricky. It was Trevor's affair that had changed those plans, after all.

'That right there is why I couldn't,' she said, taking the safe route. 'I wanted to have something I'd earned myself.' She paused. 'Why are you saying this?'

His expression didn't change. 'I just didn't know Bishop Enterprises had been an option for you.'

'And you're romanticising the idea of it,' she said as she realised it.

'No,' he denied, frowning. There was a pause. 'But if you worked for your father,' he said quietly, 'you might not have asked for the divorce to focus on your business.'

Her brain took his words, processed them, coached her on how to respond. But the message never reached her mouth. Her throat felt as if her voice box had been crushed. Her tongue felt thick. Her lips felt frozen.

She took a deep breath through her mouth, hoping the air would revive all the parts of her insides that had been affected by his admission.

Then, calmly—she hoped—she said, 'I probably would have worked harder if it was for my father.' She swept her tongue over her teeth. 'It's a tad hypocritical for you to stand there and tell me work wouldn't have been an issue in our marriage. You weren't home a lot. And you have the success to show for it,' she said hurriedly, not wanting to get stuck on that remark. 'You went from being an intern at my father's company to his number two in nine years. That's amazing, particularly considering the size of Bishop Enterprises.'

It had always been part of what she'd admired in him. His drive. His focus. She hadn't admired how much of that drive, that focus, he'd neglected to channel into their marriage. She'd focused so completely on her own job because Wyatt had been so focused on his. He wasn't going to turn her into the wife who waited at home for her husband. Summer refused to be the wife whose husband couldn't figure out what was more important to him: his marriage or his work.

She'd seen that happen with her mother. The end result had been her father having an affair. Summer couldn't bear for that to be her path, too. So she'd worked just as hard as Wyatt did. She'd turned her tiny brokerage into one of the most successful in the city. She might have done so at the expense of her marriage, but then, Wyatt had done that with his work, too.

At least this way, Summer had had a choice.

She'd chosen to focus on work. She hadn't been coerced into the part of the sidelined wife. The outsider because of someone else's decisions.

'I had to work hard, Summer,' he said after a while. 'I had to thank your father for taking a chance on me.'

What about me? she wanted to ask. She didn't. It was selfish to worry about herself when she understood why Wyatt felt indebted. She hadn't before they'd got married. She'd thought his loyalty to her father had been gratitude. She'd only realised the extent of it when he'd told her the truth about his childhood...

The day after their wedding.

They'd eloped with only Autumn and her then boyfriend Hunter as their witnesses, telling her parents when they were already on their way to their honeymoon. She hadn't needed either of her parents' approval—why, when they didn't care about hers?—though they'd both wholeheartedly approved.

Which had annoyed her *just* a little.

When she and Wyatt had arrived in Mauritius, at the beachfront dinner the resort had arranged for them, Wyatt had told her about his parents. She'd always known they weren't in the picture, but she'd never known the details of it until that night. Since they'd only been dating six months before their quickie marriage, she'd known there had been things both of them had kept from the other. She hadn't paid too much heed to the fact that she hadn't known all the details.

She wished she had.

'I know.' She folded her arms. She wasn't sure if it was for comfort or to keep him from noticing she wasn't wearing a bra. 'I know you feel like you owe a lot to my father.'

There was a pause.

'You make that sound like a criticism.'

Since there was no good option for her to go with, she didn't reply.

His eyes narrowed. 'Something happened between the two of you, didn't it?'

She bit her lip. Lifted a shoulder.

'I hope it isn't because of me.'

'No.'

He let out a breath. 'Good. I can't imagine if after all he's done for me...' He trailed off. 'What? Why are you looking at me like that?'

'You're not worried that my relationship with my father is strained because you're worried about me,' she said, unable to stop herself. 'You're worried because of *him*. Of what he might think of you.'

It made her want to fall to her knees and weep.

'No,' he said, taking a step towards her. She shook her head. He stopped moving. 'No, I meant—'

'It doesn't matter, Wyatt,' she interrupted desperately.

She didn't want to go there, but all the little talks

she'd given herself about staying away from the past seemed to be taunting her. In the form of her own words. In the form of her memories.

Just like that, she was back in Beijing again, the maître d' querying about her mother.

'My mother?' Summer asked, confused.

'Petite, short curly brown hair?' the maître d' clarified. 'She was with your father when they stayed here about a year ago? I'm sorry,' she added, 'of course you can't remember. The only reason I do is because it was the day before my maternity leave and she was so lovely to me. And so affectionate with your father! I remember hoping my husband and I still felt that way about each other when we're their age.'

Her confusion had had nothing to do with the time between that night and now. It had been because her mother was neither petite, nor did she have short, curly brown hair. Her world had slowed down and time had frozen as she'd realised her mother wasn't the woman the maître d' had been talking about.

That assumption had been made based on whoever that woman had been and her father's *affection* for one another. And, she only imagined, on the fact that her father had still been wearing his wedding ring. Presumably, the petite brown-haired woman had been wearing hers, too.

But it couldn't have been what she thought, she'd told herself. When her father had joined her at their table, she'd been too shocked to play coy. She'd asked him about it.

And everything had fallen apart.

Perhaps she could have accepted it if it hadn't extended beyond that. Sadly, it had. So much else in her life had fallen apart because of that night. How she felt in her family. Her career plans, though she'd somehow managed to salvage that. Her life with the man she'd loved though…

And here he was, standing in front of her, trying not only to please the man who'd put her through this, but to *imitate* him. He'd succeeded, too. Far better than he could ever know. Trevor had forced her to isolate herself from her family; Wyatt had forced her to isolate herself from him.

'Summer? What's wrong?'

She only then realised a sound had come out of her mouth. She wasn't sure what it had been, but since she'd been in pain—since she still felt it throbbing in her body—she understood the worry in Wyatt's voice.

And why, seconds later, he was in front of her, his hands gripping her arms.

'Oh.' She swallowed, blinked, turned to face him. 'I'm okay.'

'You're not okay.'

Her mouth opened to deny it, but, despite everything, all she wanted to do was lean forward so she could rest her head against his chest.

For once she didn't bother fighting what she wanted.

As soon as her head made contact, she felt his body stiffen. Knew why. She was touching him. Not only that; she was asking him for *comfort*. There was no point in denying it. Or the fact that she still found comfort in his arms, even though he was part of the reason why she needed it.

But for one short moment, Summer wanted to be comforted. She didn't want to think about how tired she was of being the only one who knew the whole truth. Or how she was the only one suffering for it.

She wanted to go back to the time when she didn't feel so alone. The last time that had happened was with Wyatt. Before he'd told her about his broken family. And how grateful he was to be a part of hers. She'd gone right back to feeling lonely then; the Wyatt who'd understood her had disappeared before her eyes.

She wouldn't get him back. She couldn't risk trying. Trying would involve telling him her family was broken, too. It would rob him of the life he'd always wanted.

The life she knew was a lie.

Summer pressed her face deeper into Wyatt's chest.

This was…disturbing.

Which was frightening, since *disturbing* wasn't

a description Wyatt had thought he'd ever use for Summer. Unless he was describing her beauty. Or her ability to make him forget why relationships never worked out, resulting in impromptu proposals and weddings.

But a show of emotion from the Queen of Control herself? That *was* disturbing. And explained why his arms were folding around her soft body instead of pushing her away.

He should have. He should have acted like a complete jerk and pushed her away. *Run* away, for his self-preservation. Instead, he was diving headfirst into the vulnerability that had made him fall for her in the first place.

He remembered it all too well, that day at the Bishops' annual Christmas party. It had been the first time he'd built up the courage to go. Before that year, he'd believed he'd needed to prove himself to Trevor before he could attend such an intimate event. Or any event Trevor had hosted. It had been an excuse, even his younger self had suspected, though for what, he hadn't been—and still wasn't—sure of.

That year he'd brought on his third and biggest client to Bishop Enterprises: Callahan Farms. Rumours had been going around for months that one of the biggest providers of pecan nuts to the Western Cape—and one of the biggest suppliers in South Africa—had been looking for someone to manage the exportation of their nuts abroad.

Wyatt had known that if the rumours had been true, he had to score them as a client. His place at Bishop Enterprises would be secure then and he'd finally be able to thank Trevor for all the other man had done for him.

He'd done the work and found out the rumours had been true.

Weeks later, Callahan Farms had become a client of Bishop Enterprises.

So that year, he'd attended the Christmas party. He'd met Autumn almost immediately upon his arrival; Summer had been missing, which Trevor had seemed faintly annoyed by. But Wyatt had met her eventually, hours into the party, sitting on the steps in the west wing of the Bishop mansion.

She'd stood immediately. 'No one is supposed to be here.'

'I'm sorry, I was—'

He'd broken off, because the beginning of his excuse had already been formulated the moment he'd seen someone sitting on the stairs. That had been the part that had come out smoothly.

The rest had died on his lips because he had been too in awe of Summer's beauty.

'You were?' she prompted, taking the last steps down until she was on the ground level, walking to him.

'I was,' he repeated, before figuring out he was acting like an idiot. He cleared his throat. 'Sorry, I think I got lost.'

She dropped her head. 'On the other side of the house to where the party is?'

He winced. 'Fine, you caught me. I was exploring. This is—' He broke off, shaking his head.

She gave a sparkly laugh, though there was something hoarse in the sound that had his eyes resting on her face.

'Yeah, I know. It is...' Her mouth curved. 'Summer, by the way.'

'Yeah, I know.' He'd seen pictures, but it hadn't at all prepared him for the reality. 'You're the other sister.' He winced again. 'Sorry.'

'Don't worry,' she replied with a small smile. 'It's not inaccurate. Who are you?'

'Oh, yeah, sorry.' He cleared his throat. Again. 'Wyatt Montgomery.'

'Nut Boy,' she said with a smirk.

He blinked. 'I'm sorry—what?'

Her smile widened. 'You're the man who secured Callahan Farms for my father? You know, the man who charmed Pete Callahan into allowing Bishop Enterprises to sell his nuts abroad.'

He smiled. Stepped closer to her. 'I guess I am Nut Boy, then.'

'Nice to meet you,' she said, taking another step towards him.

It was the first time he'd seen her eyelashes were wet, clumped together as if she had been—

As if she had been crying.

His heart had collapsed at her feet.

She wasn't crying now though. He knew it because her body was absolutely still in his arms. The only reason he assumed she still wanted him to comfort her—*if* that was what she wanted—was the fact that she was still there.

Unable to resist, he rested his head on top of hers, taking in the smell of coconut and shea butter of her hair. She hadn't loosened it for her nighttime stroll, though it wasn't in the stern hairstyle she'd worn earlier that day. She'd wrapped it in a silk scarf, so that the top of her curls was visible while keeping them away from her face.

The smell of her, the feel of her, sent an intense wave of longing through him. And now he understood some of the anger that had kept him from going to bed that night. A lot of other nights over the past two years, too, he thought.

She'd given up on this. On the fact that they could stand in each other's arms and not know what was wrong, but still comfort one another. It was a small thing, this, and it was one of many, but it cut through him easily. As if the thought had been specially designed to cut through him.

He pushed it aside when she pulled back.

'I'm sorry.'

She wasn't looking at him again. Which hadn't ever been something she'd done before, but he recognised as a tactic. A protective tactic; to protect herself from *him*.

'You don't have to apologise,' he said. 'I get it.'

'No, you don't.'

'No, I don't,' he agreed. 'But the chances of you telling me are slim, so I won't even ask.'

There was a long silence.

'I was…remembering.'

His heart thudded hard against his chest as he thought about the look on her face before she'd gone into his arms. The way her expression had twisted, tightened, and then fallen in what could only have been pain. What was she remembering?

Hope he hadn't known existed inside him inflated, swelling even more when she looked up at him and there was longing in her eyes.

They looked at each other for a long time, and though he knew it probably wasn't the best idea to let it linger, he did. He let the connection soothe the hurt inside him. Felt it skim over a deeper, darker hurt he'd refused to listen to.

Now wasn't the time to listen to it either, and yet he did, unable not to. The hurt about his father's abandonment was simple. One day Wyatt had come home from school and the man was no longer there. He'd always been there when Wyatt had got home. He'd worked the late shift at the pharmacy to look after Wyatt until Wyatt's mother had got home in the evenings.

That day, Wyatt had panicked. His father hadn't been there, but his clothes had been. At ten years old, Wyatt hadn't completely understood that someone could leave without their clothes. Then he'd found the note—the *Tell the kid I'm sorry* note—and even his ten-year-old brain had been able to comprehend that. It had even linked his father's behaviour the weeks before to his father leaving.

The coolness; the distance. Almost exactly how Summer had begun to act before she'd left, too.

Then there was the hurt about his mother. That was darker. More complicated. More...

More.

He couldn't think through it, or over it, as easily he did with his father. For some reason, it stuck in his head in the same way the hurt he felt about Summer leaving did.

Or perhaps, all the hurt had meshed together and now he couldn't figure out what was what.

He stepped back at the unexpectedness of it, the arms he hadn't realised were still around Summer's waist dropping to his sides as his hands clenched into fists. Suddenly it wasn't a summer's night at a lodge next to the beach. He wasn't holding his ex-wife under the stars with the sound of the sea crashing against the shore somewhere in the distance.

There was only the hurt.

It stiffened his body, had him straightening his spine. He gave a slight shake of his head when Summer sent him a questioning look. Her expression instantly went blank—the mask had returned.

They both took a step away from one another.

He nodded his head now, and she turned, correctly interpreting his signal and moving ahead of him.

He swallowed, trying to ignore how it felt as if he'd been turned inside out.

It didn't work.

CHAPTER FIVE

It took Summer a full hour to get out of bed.

She'd struggled to fall asleep, and at some point during the night she'd opened her curtains so she could be calmed by the waves splashing against the pillars that held her cabin up. It was gorgeous, her cabin. It had stained oak laminate flooring; white wooden panels that formed the V of its roof; chequered carpets in the middle of each of the floors; and the glass sliding doors that made up the entire wall facing the ocean.

She and Autumn would be sharing for the weekend. Since Autumn was only arriving the next day, Summer had the room to herself. She was lucky. If Autumn saw her now, she'd take one look at—

Her phone rang. Autumn was video calling her. *Great.*

Summer sat up, brushed a finger over her eyebrows to straighten them. She didn't bother with her hair; it was in her silk sleep scarf anyway. Attempts to fix it would be futile. At least if she wanted to avoid Autumn bombarding her with messages about why she wasn't answering.

'Hi,' Summer said when she answered.

'Hi,' Autumn replied. Summer recognised her sister's bakery in the background, which meant Autumn was likely calling during a coffee break. 'You've just woken up?'

'What makes you think that?' Summer asked. 'Is it my amazing outfit?' She tilted the phone so Autumn could see the nightshirt she wore. She tried to forget Wyatt had seen and held her in it, too. 'Or is it my fashion-forward headscarf?' She straightened the phone again.

'Both are fabulous, but I'm going to go out on a limb here and say you're not wearing that to Mom and Dad's fancy breakfast?'

She groaned.

Autumn frowned. 'You forgot about it?'

'No,' she said defensively. A second later she said, 'I'm avoiding it.'

'Summer,' Autumn said in that tone she used when she was annoyed but pretending not to be. 'You can't be there and not attend the festivities.'

'Hmm.'

'Hey.' Autumn sat down on the bench outside the bakery. 'You said you were going to give this a try.'

'Because it means so much to you.'

'It doesn't mean anything to you?'

She didn't reply.

'Sun,' Autumn said after a moment, using her childhood nickname for Summer.

Autumn had come up with it after Summer

had started calling her 'Wind'. It had been a joke because Autumn was a whirlwind of goodness. Successful, perfect. Determined to be the best at everything she did. Besides, it had seemed fitting, considering the season Autumn had been named after.

Her nickname had a similar origin story.

It had been their little joke, until one day Autumn had told Summer she felt as if Summer was the sun for her. Bright. Warm. Autumn was the only one who still described her that way. *Sun* was more suited to the person Summer had been before her father's deception. Before she'd been forced to lie to her sister.

'Mom and Dad are going to renew their vows tomorrow,' Autumn was saying. 'They'd really love for it to be a new beginning for our entire family as well. If you—'

'Wait,' Summer interrupted. 'Did you just say *they'd* really love it? As in, they spoke to you about this?'

Autumn's eyes widened. 'I… Well…' She went quiet for a moment. 'We were out to dinner—' this part wasn't a surprise; Autumn had been honest about seeing their parents for a monthly dinner. Summer had politely declined her sister's invitation '—and they'd mentioned how much they'd missed you. The real you,' Autumn said when Summer opened her mouth, 'not whoever you are around them.'

Or around you.

'Dad, too?' she asked. Autumn nodded.

There was a pause.

'It's been eight years,' Summer said. 'Why now?'

'I don't know.'

'Do you really not know? Or did they ask you not to tell me?'

The confusion in Autumn's eyes was genuine. 'No, they didn't.' A beat passed. 'Why would you ask me that? They'd never expect me to keep something from you.'

Summer didn't reply.

'Sun,' Autumn said slowly, 'what's going on?'

'Nothing,' Summer said.

But if she needed proof this weekend was messing with her head, Summer now had it. Not once since the affair had she given any indication that she'd known about it before her mother and sister had. Not once in *eight years*. Within minutes into this phone call though, she had.

'Is this why you called?' Summer said, changing the subject. 'To check on my behaviour?'

Autumn searched Summer's face, then she shook her head. 'No, actually. I was wondering if you were okay. About the family stuff and the, um…' Autumn hesitated. 'The Wyatt stuff.'

'What Wyatt stuff?' Summer asked immediately. Brightly.

Autumn snorted. 'That's not going to work on me, sis.'

'What isn't going to work on you?' she asked in the faux bright tone that made her own ears bleed. 'I have no idea what you're talking about, Autumn. I am perfectly fine. But I must dash because I am terribly late for a fancy breakfast.'

She blew her sister a kiss before Autumn could protest, and ended the call. Seconds later her phone flashed with a message.

You used posh words. And a British accent. You're not fooling me.

And seconds after that:

I'll be there in twenty-four hours. Hang on until then?

Summer softened at the question, and typed back.

I can do that.

Autumn replied:

And don't do anything I wouldn't do while you do.

Summer smirked, and sent back a laughing emoticon, then a heart one.

Summer knew Autumn had been checking in

because she was concerned. It was the same reason she was doing recon—reconciliation, in this case—work for their parents.

Autumn had never been able to understand why Summer couldn't move on from it as the rest of them had. It was because Summer couldn't tell her the truth: not only had their father cheated, but he'd asked Summer to keep it a secret for months. *Months.*

He'd told her it was because of business. He had an important deal to close, and he didn't want to complicate things by focusing on a personal issue. He'd put business above their family, and he'd had no reservations asking Summer to do the same.

It had made her physically ill. For those two months, Summer's stomach had twisted and knotted. She hadn't been able to eat. She hadn't been able to be in her family's company either. The affair had been an ominous cloud promising a storm, following her everywhere. And she couldn't warn the people she cared about to prepare for it. Every time she was with them, she wanted to tell them to check the shelter. To bring an umbrella at the very least.

But she was caught between the business and her family, too. No, not the business and the family; her father, and her mother and sister. At that point, she'd been closer to her father than to her mother. Maybe she'd still been protecting him when she'd agreed to keep the affair a secret. Or maybe she hadn't wanted to deal with the aftermath of her family finding out about her father's affair.

All she knew was that it was the worst two months of her life. So when her stomach had begun twisting and knotting again in her marriage—when she hadn't been able to eat and she'd seen Wyatt put business above his family, too—she'd tried to protect herself. She'd thought she had. But seeing him now didn't make her feel so sure.

In fact, it brought back all her memories of their marriage. At first, things had been good. They had spent time together, and Wyatt would easily put off work for another hour with her. But then Bishop Enterprises had nearly lost Wyatt's biggest client and things had changed. Wyatt had spent more time at work. When he'd been home, he was working. Talking to her father. And as Wyatt had worked himself into the ground to prove himself to Trevor—to himself, too, she thought—he'd changed.

She'd withdrawn into herself so she wouldn't feel how much it hurt. In some ways it had been easy. She'd already perfected the cool, disinterested mask with her family. Convincing herself that she had to be cool and disinterested with her husband, too, had been simple. Painful though, since he'd been the first person since her father's affair to see behind the mask she'd worn. She'd felt understood for the first time in years.

Until she hadn't been.

Her concern now was that this little holiday was cracking her mask. Hell, after last night, with Wyatt, she was worried it might have already broken.

But it couldn't be. She would have to glue any broken pieces back together, paint over any cracks. She couldn't let her family know the truth. She couldn't let Wyatt know the truth. She was more worried about that last part, because she'd always been vulnerable around him. Vulnerable Summer told Wyatt things he shouldn't know. Last night was the perfect example.

If she told Wyatt the truth, the work he'd found his purpose in would look different. And he needed that purpose. He hadn't had it growing up, and his life had looked dramatically different. He was proud of what he'd achieved now. She wouldn't tell him he'd achieved it at the expense of their family. She wouldn't taint that purpose for him.

She thought she did a pretty good job of fixing the mask when she finally joined breakfast. Her mother had arranged it for all their guests on the terrace of their significantly larger cabin.

'How lovely of you to join us, dear,' her mother said when Summer arrived.

The words would seem genuine to anyone who was not Lynette Bishop's daughter. Why would they be familiar with the *you've embarrassed me in front of people and we shall discuss this later* voice?

'I'm so sorry, Mother,' Summer said smoothly,

pressing a kiss to her mother's cheek. After a
brief moment of hesitation, she did the same with
her father. The kiss, the hesitation, felt strange.
Hopefully no one would notice. She intentionally
avoided Wyatt's gaze.

'I struggled to sleep last night so I tried to catch
an extra hour this morning.'

'Did you?' her mother asked, her voice softening as her eyes swept over Summer's face.

'I did,' Summer answered with a smile. 'Now,
why don't you catch me up on what the activities
for the day are?'

She listened to her mother's plans, ignoring the
interested looks the other guests gave her. Most im-
portantly, she ignored Wyatt's gaze. She could feel
it on her as acutely as she could his arms around
her body from the night before. It was almost as if
his *look at me* bet had been issued again.

'Did you say— Did you say *disco*, Mom?' she
asked, snapping to attention.

Lynette's smile brightened. 'I said some other
things, too—' her eyebrow lifted, informing Summer she knew her daughter hadn't been paying
attention '—but yes, we end tonight off with a
disco.'

Summer wrinkled her nose. 'Can't we call it a
dance?'

A chuckle went through the guests, and Lynette's expression turned into genuine amusement.
Summer didn't even look at her father. Partly be-

cause she knew his reaction wouldn't be genuine, and partly because she was still angry about what Autumn had told her. How dared he tell Autumn he missed the real Summer? *He* was the reason that Summer no longer existed.

Sometimes she'd find herself staring at him, wondering if the man who'd so patiently taught her the ins and outs of the Bishop business was still there. That man had been honest. He wouldn't have lied. He wouldn't have asked her to lie.

She shook it off.

'You won't understand this, I'm sure, but discos were popular in my day.'

'Your day is right now, Mother,' Summer said sweetly. 'I've never met another woman as on top of current events as you are.'

'Oh, you're sucking up.' Lynette winked at her. 'I like it.'

There was another round of laughter before someone asked her mother about where the disco would be held. Summer let a breath out through her lips when the question distracted her mother, then made the mistake of looking at Wyatt. He was frowning at her. She immediately lowered her gaze, knowing what he must be thinking.

She was trying hard to make their family seem normal. She'd done it before. And she was sure that to most of her parents' guests, she was succeeding. But she could still feel Wyatt's gaze on her. He'd seen her let out that breath after joking with her mother, as if the joking hadn't come naturally. She was sure he'd noticed her hesitation before kissing her father, as if it was something she didn't do on a regular basis.

He'd already picked up on something between her and her father the day before. He was definitely looking. She thought he might be seeing, too…

It instantly had her wondering if she'd fixed the mask as well as she'd thought she had. But a deeper, more destructive part of her wondered if the old Wyatt was back. The man who'd seen through her façade. The one she'd fallen for in the first place…

Summer.

She had to up her game.

There was a break between breakfast and the lake cruise her mother had arranged. Summer used it to take a walk on the beach. She hoped it would give her back her steadiness. But when she heard footsteps behind her on the wooden path that led down to the beach, she gritted her teeth.

'Summer,' a voice said, and her feet stopped of their own accord. Then her father was next to her, and Summer didn't know what to do.

'Do you mind if I take a walk with you?'

Summer swallowed. 'I was hoping to have some alone time.'

'I won't keep you long, I promise.'

Unable to say no, she nodded, and they continued the walk down in silence. She wondered what he wanted, and, if it was nothing, why he'd come at all. She felt the tension grow in her shoulders with each step down; she could have done without that. In fact, she could have done without all of it, which was probably why she was hoping for something unrealistic like her father joining her without wanting to talk.

It hadn't always been unrealistic. She could remember instances when she and Trevor would walk together. Mostly during summer vacations. Largely to talk about the business. But it had been bonding time. And it had been enough for her.

She missed it.

Her heart ached at the surprise of it. At the longing of it.

She angled a look to the side. When she saw Trevor was looking out at the ocean and not at her, she allowed herself to look at him more freely. He'd grown older quickly. Or perhaps she thought that because she didn't dare study him if she could help it.

His grey hair was stark against his brown skin, his tall frame slowly hunkering over itself with age. He was still a handsome man, and one of those annoying kinds whose age made them more attractive somehow. She wondered if he'd be more or less likely to cheat because of it.

The thought caused a lump in her throat to grow, which, of course, was part of the problem with her relationship with her father. She'd found insidious little things like that creeping into her thoughts all the time. Even when she wasn't anywhere close to thinking about what her father had done. It made her feel as though she couldn't trust herself. Or him.

She rubbed absently at an ache in her chest.

'I wanted to talk to you about this weekend,' her father said finally. She made a non-committal sound. 'I know it's hard for you to be here.'

She still didn't respond; she knew this was a trick. No matter what she said, it would open her up to this line of conversation. The one about her feelings about what had happened.

Too little, too late.

'I've let this sit much longer than I should have,' Trevor said. 'I think a part of me hoped that we'd move past it like the rest of the family has.'

'Not a part,' Summer corrected. 'The whole of you, or it would have taken a lot less time than it has for you to mention this to me.'

Trevor sighed. 'Do you blame me for not wanting to relive the most shameful mistake in my past?'

'Yes, I do. But wait—which mistake?' she asked. 'Sleeping with a woman who wasn't your wife? Putting your business above your family? Or asking me to keep quiet about it? Doesn't matter,' she said over whatever he would have said. 'I blame you for all of it.'

She stopped walking, her feet digging into the sand. It was warm from the sun. Summer wished the heat could rise from her toes up, into her heart, so she wouldn't feel so cold.

'Are we done now?' Summer asked, turning to face her father. He'd stopped walking, too. She ignored the pain on his face. The surprise.

'I didn't realise...' He trailed off. 'You think I put the business over our family?'

She laughed, hard and harsh. 'You're not asking me that question because you want to know the answer. You already know it's true.'

He didn't reply.

She laughed again. 'Of course you know it's true. Because you remember what you said to me when I found out about the affair.' His eyes widened; he did. She would force him to hear it anyway. 'You told me you didn't want to focus on a personal issue like this when you had a business deal to concentrate on.' She paused. 'But, please, Dad, tell me how that makes me more important than work? Or Mom and Autumn, for that matter?'

Again, there was silence.

'Are you regretting telling Autumn you'd like to see the real me now?'

'Summer,' he said slowly. 'I didn't think... I didn't know...' He took a breath. 'I told you I was sorry—'

'No,' Summer interrupted, her eyes suddenly feeling hot. 'You actually haven't.'

Her father blinked. 'No, Sun, I... I did.'

'Don't call me that,' Summer said immediately, the heat prickling and her throat thickening again.

At what her father had said. At what she'd said. At the fact that she didn't mean it. Not really. Not when something inside her had turned at the name she hadn't heard come from his lips in over eight years.

'I'm sorry,' he said hoarsely. 'About everything.'

She stared at him, and a part of her wished she could accept the apology. But she couldn't. Not when he thought an apology like that was adequate.

Not when she doubted he knew what he was apologising for.

'The worst part is that you don't see why I can't move past it,' she told him, her voice breaking. 'You think it's because I can't get over the affair. But it's because I can't get over you asking me not to turn to the people I love after finding out. You pushed me to the outside of the family, Dad. Now you're wondering why I can't just step back in.' She swallowed. 'There are a lot of barriers keeping me from doing that. You built most of them.'

She took a deep breath.

'I'll see you at the boat,' she said. 'Don't worry. No one will suspect a thing.'

She turned and headed back for the lodge.

He hadn't meant to spy. That was what it was called, right? Watching people without hearing their words?

Though in all honesty, Wyatt didn't need to hear the words to know what was happening. From his position at the top of the pathway that led to the beach, he could see the tight hold of Trevor's shoulders; the angry expression on Summer's face. The sadness there, too, Wyatt thought. The hurt.

It hadn't been his intention to spy. He'd only wanted to talk with Summer about the night before. She'd been late to breakfast, which had prevented him from speaking to her beforehand. He suspected that had been the reason for her tardiness. Then she'd rushed off so quickly afterwards that he'd had to run after her—only to see Trevor had got there first.

He'd thought about waiting for them to be done before he'd been caught by the stiffness in Summer's posture. He forgot about his own intentions and watched as they spoke. As they *argued*. There was definitely something going on between Summer and Trevor.

He couldn't dwell on it when Summer turned around and began walking back to the lodge. He immediately turned and walked to the rendezvous point for the lake cruise, not willing to be caught in the act. He made it there earlier than the rest of the guests, and spent his entire time waiting wondering what the hell he'd just seen.

It was a refreshing difference from the thoughts that had kept him up the night before. Or was it the effort not to think about those thoughts that had kept him up? Probably both. Either way, this was much more interesting than the dark pits of his feelings about his mother. About his longing for his ex-wife.

Not that thinking about Trevor and Summer helped him figure out what was happening between them.

Summer's behaviour towards her father now was starkly different from when they'd been married. Or was it? Thinking back now, he couldn't remember too many occasions where he'd seen Summer and Trevor interact. When they had, he couldn't remember those interactions being anything other than respectful.

He hadn't paid that much attention to it, if he was being honest. A lot of the time his thoughts had been on work.

Because you know I was only taking my cue from you. Working hard. Focusing on building a name for myself.

Summer's words bounced into his mind, dribbling there until he paid attention to why he remembered them. Was it possible he'd missed something because of his work? Had he been so involved he hadn't noticed Summer didn't have a good relationship with her father, even then?

He dismissed the thought instantly. The Bishops didn't have bad relationships with one another. They were stable. They made jokes. Showed affection. None of that said *bad relationship.* And he would know. He had as bad a relationship with his family as they came. Besides, he'd been a part of the Bishop family. Whatever had happened must have been after his and Summer's divorce.

Or were you so enthralled by the idea of the Bishops that you didn't see the reality?

Lynette joined him then, smiling brightly when she saw him waiting, and he couldn't think about the answer.

But the question lingered.

'Bless you for being here before me, Wyatt.'

Wyatt tilted his head. 'You're…welcome?'

Lynette laughed. 'It makes me feel less embarrassed about how excited I've been feeling about this weekend. If you're here before me, you must be enthusiastic?'

Wyatt smiled. 'You have nothing to be embarrassed about, Mrs Bishop. I think it's nice that you and Trevor are still so in love.'

Something on Lynette's face tightened, then softened. 'We've been through enough to know what's important.' Her gaze sharpened on his. 'Do you?'

Wyatt didn't get the chance to answer when Lynette's friend joined them. Lynette gave him a nod and began to talk about the cruise, leaving Wyatt to figure out—again—what had happened.

He thought about what he would have answered if he'd had to. Yes, he knew? Stability, security.

Happiness, love. Lynette might have been happy with that answer. For some reason, he was not.

Because he'd tried it? Followed the example of the man who had it all and he'd failed?

But *he* hadn't failed. He just hadn't been good enough for the woman he'd thought he could find those things with.

He stopped himself. That line of thought was about as productive as what he'd been thinking about—or trying not to think about—the night before.

As if you weren't thinking about Summer last night, too.

The image of her in that loose nightshirt, the flimsy jersey over it, flashed through his mind. He tried to shake it off. It was successful only because she arrived then, in a bright dress that reminded him of the very season she was named after.

Her eyes fluttered over to him, and she gave him a slight nod. A surprise, considering how she'd avoided looking at him that morning at breakfast. Except for that one moment, which seemed similar to how she was looking to him now. As if she needed to. As if it…steadied her.

She stayed towards the back of the group, putting a solid distance between her and the rest of the guests. She had a large straw hat in one hand, which she clutched so tightly he thought she might break it. He walked over to her side, pretending not to hear her sharp exhalation when he stopped.

'I take it you're not looking forward to this?'

'What?' she asked, then gave him a smile so fake he expected it to appear on a plastic surgery TV show. 'I'm excited to be here. I love cruises.'

His lips spread as he listened to her. By the time she was done, he was chuckling.

'Man, you hate this so much.'

She gave him a look, before letting out a small laugh of defeat. 'Is it that obvious?'

'You mean is your extremely poor acting revealing your displeasure? Yes,' he informed her, without waiting for an answer. She looked up, shook her shoulders.

'Okay. Okay,' she said again. Then she hung her head before looking at him in sorrow. 'I will pay whatever amount it takes for you to distract me for the rest of the day.'

'You… Me…'

He stopped making a fool of himself, took a breath and tried to process what she was asking.

'Summer,' he said slowly, 'are you asking me to keep you company?'

'Don't make it sound like that,' she said irritably. Which, frankly, made him feel a lot better than thinking his ex-wife had been kidnapped by aliens. This was much more…on brand for her than asking something from him.

'I'm surprised.'

'Exactly. That's what you're making it sound like.'

'Because it's the truth,' he exclaimed and she swatted his arm with her hat.

'Keep your voice down,' she said in a low voice. 'I don't want the world to know I'm asking you a favour.'

'You're asking me a *favour*?'

Something remarkably like a moan slipped from her lips. She straightened her shoulders and looked him dead in the eye.

'I understand your surprise. Plus, you're correct; those words would never have left my lips if my sister was here.' She took a deep breath. 'Unfortunately, she isn't, and I cannot, for the life of me, pretend to be excited to attend a cruise with a bunch of people I don't particularly care for.'

She'd said all those words while exhaling, and was now taking another deep breath.

Wyatt braced himself for more.

'You're the only person I know here. Or I'm comfortable with.' She pulled a face. 'Relatively,' she added, before letting out a huff of air. 'It's not ideal, I know, but, for one day, can we set the stuff between us aside and be friends?'

She blinked—once, twice, three times—and opened her mouth. Closed it. Then met his gaze.

She was the one who looked surprised now. As if she had no idea what had come out of her mouth. As if she didn't recognise herself in what she'd asked him.

He felt the corners of his mouth tug up, and the

What the hell is happening? feeling he'd had faded behind something more intense. Something that straightened out the bumps of hurt and anger that had initially kept him from saying yes.

Affection. And the desire to give her whatever she wanted.

Not that he'd make it easy for her.

'What is happening,' he said deliberately, 'is called humility.'

'What are you talking about?'

'It's this thing that allows you to ask other people for stuff, and not depend only on yourself.'

'Wyatt,' she said after a moment, 'are you really using this as an opportunity to teach me a moral lesson?'

'Hey—' he lifted his hands '—this isn't the kind of moment that comes around every day. I have to capitalise on it.'

She stared at him, slowing moving her head from side to side, though he didn't think she knew she was doing it.

'This is what I get for asking you for help,' she muttered.

He didn't resist the smile. 'It is.'

She glowered at him. 'You're not even telling me whether you're going to help me.'

'You still want me to?' he asked innocently. 'After what you just went through?'

'Wyatt,' she said, in what was definitely a moan. 'They're beginning to climb on the boat. If you don't give me an answer, I'm going to have to sit with someone I don't know and…' her voice dropped '…*socialise.*'

He laughed again, and a voice in his head told him to enjoy the feeling while he could. It probably wouldn't last long. Which gave him an idea.

'Fine, I'll do it.'

She brightened. 'Thank—'

'On one condition.'

What?' she asked flatly.

'I get to ask you one question.'

'What kind of question?' Her expression had gone careful, and now the voice in his head was telling him he was messing with things he shouldn't be messing with.

'Any question.' He lifted a hand before she could protest. 'Those are my terms.'

'Wyatt? Summer?'

They both turned their heads. For the first time, Wyatt saw that they were the only guests not on the boat. He also saw the interested expression on Lynette's face; the unreadable one on Trevor's, who stood just behind his wife.

'Are you two coming?' Lynette asked.

They looked at each other, and Summer sucked in her lip. What felt like an eternity later, she nodded.

'Deal.'

CHAPTER SIX

SUMMER DIDN'T KNOW what had come over her. Her first answer was desperation. It rang true, and louder, than any of the others, and she went with it. Which, all things considered, was a relief. She didn't want to think about the other reasons she might have asked Wyatt to be her friend.

Her friend. Oh, the sound of it made her cringe. But she'd been on a roll, and she hadn't paused to think about what she was saying. If she had, she wouldn't have done it. And he hadn't interrupted her—which made her wonder if he was giving her the opportunity to embarrass herself—so she'd kept talking and now she was sitting next to him on a boat.

It was actually nice. The boat had seats along its edge, with about ten more in pairs of two down the middle, separated by a bar. It seated all thirty of the guests—thirty-two, including her parents—comfortably, and the crew of three were in a small cabin enclosed by glass towards the back of the boat. She and Wyatt sat near the cabin.

Part of the deal, she thought, and relief flowed through her. She'd dreaded the socialising this weekend would include. The pretence, too. After speaking with her father, those feelings sat like stale bread in the pit of her stomach. And she'd sought comfort from the first person who'd come to mind when she thought she needed to be comforted.

She didn't dwell on that.

The point was, she didn't feel like being nice to people. She'd have to be nicer than usual, too, to prove to her father she could pretend everything was okay. So the desperation at turning to her ex-husband had been a reasonable kind. The fact that he'd said yes, though, was…interesting.

It wasn't new. The night they'd met at the Christmas party he'd helped her go into that room of people she didn't care about and pretend to be a happy family. Of course, she'd still had to go into the room and pretend, but Wyatt had made it easier.

When he'd asked her later why she hadn't been herself, she'd been stunned. No one she'd only just met knew she wasn't being herself. They almost always thought she was just the cool, aloof sister. The distant heiress to Autumn's warm persona. She'd played the role so well even her family believed it.

Wyatt seeing through her had felt significant in a way she couldn't understand then. But she'd felt understood. Which almost made up for all the times after when he'd let her down.

She'd asked him more times than she cared to admit to help her deal with social situations. Family obligations. Work meetings. He'd always say yes, and he'd keep his word…if it pertained to those family obligations. When it didn't, like clockwork, he'd call the afternoon of the event and cancel. Something important had come up at work, he'd always say. She didn't even think he realised it. But she had. And she'd learnt to stop relying on him.

Which meant his transition into her father had been like clockwork, too.

So the fact that she was sitting next to him now was so strange. It did feel as if he was the old Wyatt. The man she'd met that first night. Shaking her head—it was best not to go down that road— she stared out at the long reeds running along the river the boat was cruising down.

Beyond the reeds were hills of varying heights, covered in large part by bushes and the occasional tree. Every now and then, Summer would spy a house between the bushes; or at the top of the hills, though those were predominant and huge, with large windows and balconies to take full advantage of the view.

Though it was hot, the movement of the boat brought a welcoming breeze that cooled the sting of the sun. Laughter floated from the front of the boat down to them, light chattering adding to the ambience.

Summer closed her eyes, tilting her head up, and enjoyed the moment.

She had no idea when the last time was that she'd had one of these moments. Where it felt as if the world had slowed down and her mind stilled because of it. She'd spent the last six years building her own business. Making it a success had felt like a necessity after she'd given up the position waiting for her at Bishop Enterprises.

She'd been studying Finance when she'd found out about her father's affair, a degree she and Trevor had agreed would make her an asset to the company. After everything had happened, though, working for her father had seemed like a cruel joke. So she'd done her research and added Portfolio Management to her degree. Owning her own brokerage had seemed like a decent career change. But if she was honest, she hated that she wasn't working for the company that bore her name.

In the beginning, that hatred had fuelled her. Her marriage failing had done the same thing. When it had failed, she'd been determined to make her business a success. It soothed the ache that she wasn't working for Bishop Enterprises. And the strange burning sensation she got in her stomach whenever she thought that Wyatt had sacrificed their marriage for the sake of the job she should have had.

Regardless, it meant world-slowing, mind-stilling moments weren't easily found. She would enjoy this.

But she opened her eyes when she felt Wyatt's gaze on her.

It was interesting how she always knew it was him.

She shifted her head and their eyes met, and again it felt as if the world slowed down. Except now, her mind didn't still, it froze. Handed over the controls of the situation to her heart, who took the reins gladly and guided Summer into noticing how handsome Wyatt was.

He wasn't the obvious kind of handsome. His face was…complicated. There were faint lines running across his forehead, his eyebrows were dark, almost severe. There was a dent in his chin that always made her think someone had pressed their finger into it and his skin had absorbed the pressure as if it were clay.

There were lines around his eyes, too, which told her his skin crinkled when he smiled. And between his eyebrows, that told her he frowned almost as much as he smiled.

There was the way his nose seemed as smooth as a slope in the Alps, leading to lips that were not quite as full as hers, but were sensuous. And the dents on either side of his mouth—his dimples—made her think she could fall into them every time they appeared.

It made complicated *very* sexy.

'You're staring at me.' His voice was lightly amused, and she lifted her eyes from his lips.

'You were staring at me first,' she said with a smile—and oh, no, she was becoming Marry-the-Man-Before-Thinking-it-Through Summer again.

'Only because I've only ever seen you with that expression on your face once before,' he said, distracting her.

'When?'

'The suntan session of two and a half years ago.'

'You mean the time I was having a relaxing afternoon on the beach and you poured a glass of ice water down my back?'

'I did not pour it down your back,' he retorted. 'I tripped over the bottle of champagne you'd left on the sand next to you.'

'So you say, Montgomery,' she said with a snort. 'But that water landed an awful lot quicker than you did, and, if memory serves me correctly, you weren't on the floor when I opened my eyes.'

'I wasn't,' he confirmed, 'because I have excellent reflexes.'

'Sure,' she said dryly.

He shrugged. 'That's my story, Bishop. It's never changed.'

'Hmm.'

She shook her head, though she was aware her lips were curved. Was even more aware his were, too.

She tried to remember the last time she and Wyatt had smiled at each other. Not grimaced, or exchanged fake gestures of politeness, but *smiled*.

Genuinely, because they were amused with one another or just…comfortable. She couldn't remember, which did something terrible to her insides.

'What's wrong?'

'Nothing,' she said immediately, automatically. There was a stretch of silence.

'When are you going to learn that you can't lie to me, Summer?' he asked quietly. 'When are you going to realise that I can see right through you?'

But you didn't, she nearly answered. *When it mattered, you didn't.*

She swallowed, clutched at her skirt, crinkling the material of it between her fingers. It was rather that than her lips, which was what she'd wanted to grip closed. To make sure she didn't say something she shouldn't. Like the fact that she hadn't wanted to divorce him; she just couldn't keep watching him turn into her father. Or feel as if he was turning her into her mother.

Or that she had felt more alone in her marriage than she had with her family.

When Wyatt had found her crying on the steps at her father's Christmas party, it was because she'd been tired of the pretence. A moment of weakness, she could admit, but it had been worth it because she'd found Wyatt. She'd kept him away from her parents in the six months before their wedding so she wouldn't have to pretend around him. And for those six months, she had been herself. She'd been happy.

She'd refused to compromise it with the truth of her father's affair.

At first, she'd made excuses. She hadn't wanted her father to be a part of her relationship. Besides, she and Wyatt had only just met. And he worked for her father, for heaven's sake. It had soon become harder. She'd fallen in love with him and had seen his respect for Trevor. After their wedding, when he'd told her about his parents, she'd realised it went far beyond respect. It was about purpose. About having something to work towards. And she'd understood that having a goal kept Wyatt moving forward instead of dwelling in his traumatic past.

She wouldn't take that away from him. No matter how much she wished his goal were better than having a life like Trevor Bishop's.

'I'll get us something to drink, okay?' Summer said, in desperate need of something to do.

Something that wasn't answering him.

Wyatt gave Summer a faint nod and watched as she moved towards the bar. She was stopped by a dark-haired woman halfway there. Her expression was pleasant—carefully so, he thought—as she leaned down to listen. A moment later she nodded, and stepped forward, before pausing and making her way to the front of the boat, where her parents were.

She spoke to them, nodded. Then she got her

phone out of her dress pocket and began to type into it. She made her way down the entire boat, speaking to each and every person, her expression now of concentration as she tapped her phone.

Only when she reached the bar and spoke with the barman, showing him her phone, did Wyatt realise she'd started taking orders from everyone on the boat. He would have laughed if he weren't so surprised. Or if she weren't coming his way again, now speaking to the people on the opposite end of the bar.

One of the men said something to her and she laughed. His surprise moved up another notch. Who was this person? Certainly not the woman who had all but begged him to keep her from talking to people? Perhaps it was that alien again.

Or perhaps it was just her.

It reminded him of that night at the Christmas party. He'd spent pretty much his entire time there with Summer. At the end of it, he'd been so reluctant to say goodbye that he'd asked her out for coffee. She'd smiled at him—one of those heart-crushing genuine smiles she had; similar, he thought suddenly, to the one she'd given him moments ago—and told him she had somewhere else to be.

'Where?' he'd asked, desperate to stay in her company.

She'd tilted her head. 'Do you want to come with me?'

'Yes,' he'd answered immediately and that smile had widened, before she'd nodded and led him to the kitchen.

There, he'd helped her pack all the leftover food into containers that had been stacked in one of the cupboards. They'd loaded them into a van she'd hired, and had taken it to a shelter where people had known her by name.

That had been the moment he'd known he was a goner.

'Can I get anything for you, sir?' Summer asked, stopping in front of him and pulling him out of the past.

'I thought you already were,' he said dryly.

'I got distracted.'

'So it seems.' He paused. 'Sparkling water, please.'

'With lemon?'

'Just the water.'

'Okay.'

She widened her eyes before heading back to the bar, giving the other orders to the barman before taking the tray the man had set out and handing it out to the first half of the boat. She did the same with the second half of the boat. Then she returned the tray to the bar before taking their drinks.

'You okay?' he asked when she sat down and handed him his.

'Fine,' she replied. 'I was stopped before I could do ours. Figured I'd just do everyone.' She winced. 'You know what I mean.'

He laughed. 'Sure.' He took a sip of his water. 'You didn't have to though.'

'No,' she agreed. 'But this way it seems like I'm interacting with everyone without really doing so. Which keeps my mother happy and makes my father believe—'

She broke off, offering him an embarrassed smile before taking a sip of her own drink. He knew she hadn't meant to say the part about her father, and he had no intention of letting it go. But he would let her think that he did. He still had his one question, and he already knew what he was going to use it on.

'That wasn't the only reason you did it,' he told her. Gratitude flashed across her face like a shooting star. It was gone just as quickly, replaced by a careful expression.

'What do you mean?'

'You do things like that for people all the time.'

'No, I don't.'

'How about that time you paid for the groceries of the woman in front of you at the store?'

'She left her purse at home. It happens to everyone.'

'The beggar you gave your lunch to after he asked for money for a loaf of bread?'

'Which one?' She shook her head. 'Doesn't matter. Anybody would have done that.'

'Or that time you—'

'Wyatt,' she interrupted him. 'Surely you have

better things to do than to repeat every good deed I've done in my life?'

He hid his smile behind the glass and watched the birds that flew over the river. He could have mentioned a lot more than he had, though he'd known she would stop him. It was as predictable as her helping people. Her generosity was rivalled only by her refusal to accept it as such.

That had been what had caught him that Saturday night at the party. The fact that she'd attended a lavish event that reeked of money and luxury, yet she'd thought of those without anything. Not only thought about them, but done something about it.

She was the most down-to-earth rich person he knew, and he'd come to know many of them in the nine years he'd built up his own wealth. She was better than even he was. That was saying something since he made sure the money he made went to helping the systems that had kept him alive when he'd been growing up.

Something inside him stilled at that thought, and he realised he needed to keep his head straight. He couldn't fall back into the man who'd spent a year falling in love with, marrying and then divorcing a woman. He'd tried that fantasy and it hadn't worked. Even realising it had him remembering that ball of pain that curled tighter and tighter into itself the more time he spent with Summer.

The time he spent remembering why he'd fallen in love with her in the first place. The time he spent watching her interact with people kindly, despite the way she felt about them. The time he spent being surprised by her, and delighted by her. The time he spent being attracted to her. Realising how perfect a match she'd been for him.

If only she'd felt the same way.

Just like that, the ball unfurled, spreading itself out in his chest and letting that pain and anger seep into his body.

CHAPTER SEVEN

WYATT STIFFENED BESIDE her. She looked over, catching her breath at the fierce expression on his face. It made his complicated features go from handsome to dangerous. It pulled at something low in her belly. Something that stretched out and purred for Dangerous Wyatt's attention.

She swallowed.

'What's wrong?' she asked, her voice hoarse.

He shook his head and she swallowed again, knowing that whatever had changed between them wouldn't get any easier if she pushed him for an answer.

She shifted, putting distance between them, but she could still feel heat radiating from his body. She could recognise it as anger, and she had no intention of putting herself in the firing line when she wasn't entirely sure what had caused it.

Though she knew it was her.

The rest of the boat trip was not as easy as the first half. She found herself looking for someone to talk to—*anything* to get away from the awkwardness happening beside her. But everyone who was available was far enough away from her that she'd have to move. Moving seemed like a concession of some kind, and she refused to concede. Even if she had no idea what she was conceding to.

Why did you have to have a wedding this weekend, Autumn? Summer asked her sister silently. She wished Autumn's bakery weren't as popular as it was. Then she felt bad, and immediately took it back. Her sister had worked her butt off to get the Taste of Autumn to where it was. Though that success wasn't a surprise. Autumn succeeded in almost everything she did. She was perfect like that.

What would Autumn have done if she'd been the one to find out about their father's affair? Would she have confronted him? Would he have asked her to keep it a secret? And would she have?

Summer stopped when the questions put a lump in her throat. When she found herself wishing it had been Autumn. She had no doubt Autumn would have done the exact right thing. She wouldn't have put herself on the outside while doing it either.

If it had been Autumn, Summer wouldn't have had a problem with Wyatt making her feel like an outsider, too. She would have put his desire to build the life he hadn't had growing up above her own hurt. Because she wouldn't have been hurt.

If it had been Autumn, Summer would have still been married.

She shut her eyes, fighting the heat of the tears that had been close ever since that conversation with her father. When she thought she'd succeeded, she opened her eyes, blowing out a small breath. But as she lifted her head, her mother looked back and caught Summer's gaze. Lynette frowned at whatever she saw on Summer's face, and suddenly the tears wouldn't stay where they were.

One trickled down her cheek, and her mother shifted forward. But Summer shook her head, offered her a smile, and then turned so that her body was facing Wyatt entirely.

'Summer?'

There was no longer danger on his face, but concern. Which made her tears want to come even faster, and she shook her head again, wiping voraciously at them before blowing out a breath and offering him a smile, too. She was suddenly immensely glad they were at the back of the boat. Not perfectly private, but enough that she didn't have to keep up with this ridiculous farce.

'You're crying,' he said softly. He brushed a thumb at a tear she'd missed.

'No, I'm not,' she corrected. 'I'm smiling. See.' She widened her smile.

His eyebrows rose. 'I don't think that expression is working as well as you think it is.'

She let out a small laugh. It sounded too much like a sob for her liking. 'A lot of things don't work as well as I think they should. As well as I would like them to.'

He studied her. 'What's wrong, Sun?'

It had been innocuous on her sister's part, using that nickname in front of Wyatt. They'd been at dinner with their parents and Autumn had used it. Summer hadn't even picked up on it, but Wyatt had asked about it after they'd given Autumn a lift home. Summer had explained it as quickly as she could.

He'd loved it. Said he felt the same way about Summer as Autumn did. Summer had no defences against it. And he knew it.

'No fair,' she said softly.

'What are you talking about?'

'Calling me that,' she said. 'You're not playing fair.'

There was a moment before he said, 'Like when you use my surname?'

'That's different.'

'How?'

'It just is.'

'Smooth.'

Summer gritted her teeth. 'Wyatt, I'm not playing a game. I'm—'

'What?' he interrupted. 'What are you doing, Sun? Because I can't see it. I don't think you can either.'

'I don't know what you're talking about.'

'But you do,' he disagreed. 'You must realise that asking me to be your *friend* today wasn't fair.'

'Now you're using my words against me.'

'Like you used what I told you about my parents against me?'

Her eyes widened. So did his.

'I'm sorry, I shouldn't have said that.'

'But you did,' she replied carefully. 'Clearly you feel it.' She paused. 'Do you feel it?'

'We shouldn't talk about this.'

'Or we should.'

'No,' he said, jaw clenched, 'we shouldn't.'

'Wyatt—'

'No, Summer,' he said in a tone inviting no discussion. 'This is not a conversation we need to have.' He met her eyes. 'It's too late. It's too late to matter.'

He repeated the words she'd told him the night before under the night sky, but he took no pleasure in doing it. Though he believed it.

What was the point in rehashing the circumstances around their break-up? It wouldn't change that they were broken up. As much as he wanted to believe that they could be friends, this boat trip had shown him why they couldn't be.

Friends couldn't be attracted to one another. They couldn't have the past hovering over them like an umbrella on a rainy day. They couldn't think about qualities that were appealing; they couldn't link those qualities to memories. To emotions.

Since all of that seemed inevitable for him around Summer, he knew they couldn't be friends.

And yet she only had to look at him, those brown eyes open wide, bright with emotion—exactly as she was looking at him now—and he seemed to forget all those reasons.

Thankfully, he didn't have to keep looking into those eyes when the captain announced the boat was once again at the marina. Since they had been sitting at the back, he and Summer got off first. He refused the crewman's help, and, despite himself, offered Summer his hand.

She looked between him and the crewman. Wyatt held his breath, as if her decision would affect the rest of his life. When she took his hand, he felt as if he'd won something. Even though the tingling in his hand had gone up his arm, straight to the most inconvenient places in his body, and told him it was not a competition.

Even though he'd just thought of all the reasons why it shouldn't be a game. Even though the fact that she'd asked for help meant nothing. Nor would it change anything. The time for change was over. She'd already made a decision that had changed everything.

Their divorce.

That decision had influenced the rest of his life. Not whose hand she took at the end of a boat trip.

'Thank you,' she said, letting go of his hand as soon as her feet were on the marina.

She brushed at that beautiful bright dress that stood out like a rainbow against her brown skin and looked at him. They stared at each other—heatedly, passionately, longingly, he didn't know—and she nodded her head to the side.

'We should probably get out of the way.'

'That would be nice, darling,' Lynette called from the boat.

Summer turned, laughed. But a blush crept up the elegant column of her neck, and there was a faint strain in her laughter. Seconds later, they both walked to an area a safe distance from the boat.

'This is getting complicated,' she said after a moment.

He angled his head, but she was looking straight ahead. Avoiding his gaze, he thought. Something about that pleased him.

It shouldn't.

I know. He nearly replied to the voice in his head. He swallowed. He was slowly losing his mental stability. Because of it, he didn't reply to Summer.

'I'm not going to force you to keep to our deal,' she continued. 'I'll survive.'

'What if I want to keep to our deal?' he asked, even though the voice in his head was still screaming at him, asking him why the hell he wasn't taking the easy way out.

'Do you?' She looked at him now. He turned to face her.

'If you keep to your end.'

'One question?'

'Yes.'

She sucked her lip under her top row of teeth, nodded. 'Fine. But only if you stay by my side for the rest of the day. We don't have to talk,' she added. 'I just don't want to talk with anyone else.'

'Not even your mother?' Lynette asked, coming towards them.

Summer's face coloured, but she said, 'Are you always eavesdropping on me, Mother?'

'I think eavesdropping implies a level of secrecy. Or stealth. I've needed neither. You've been—' her gaze drifted over to Wyatt; something akin to satisfaction flared in her eyes '—distracted.'

The colour on Summer's face deepened. 'You're making me not want to talk with you.'

'But since I birthed you and your sister naturally, despite the repeated offers of a C-section, you will.'

'You don't get to hold that over my head when I'm pretty sure you put us all in danger with that decision,' she muttered, then said more loudly to Wyatt, 'I'll catch up with you at lunch. Keep me a seat.'

Amused, and desperately trying to ignore the pleasure that went through him at her request, he nodded and walked away. He made it two metres before Trevor fell into step beside him.

'Seems like you've cut Summer quite a bit of slack,' his mentor noted.

Wyatt felt his own colour rising. 'Just doing what you asked me to.'

'And a bit more,' Trevor said. It was all he said as they made their way back to the lodge.

Wyatt wasn't entirely sure how to reply to Trevor, so he didn't say anything. It was not the first time he'd chosen that option. In fact, he'd probably done it more often than not. Despite his relationship with Trevor—despite the respect and the loyalty—there had always been something inside Wyatt that was…careful.

He didn't know why that was. Trevor had never done anything to warrant it, and Wyatt couldn't blame it on the fact that Trevor was Wyatt's ex-father-in-law. He'd known Trevor long before he'd met Summer. Though, granted, those years hadn't exactly been a walk in the park.

No, they had been hard work. Wyatt had met Trevor when he had been in his final year of his degree at university. Trevor had singled him out in class for reasons Wyatt still didn't know to this day. After his blithe answer, Trevor had told him to stay for a moment after class. Wyatt had been braced for a scolding then. Had been prepared to brush it off just as he had all the others. Instead, Trevor had offered him a summer internship.

He hadn't been able to understand it, so naturally, he'd refused. But Trevor had asked him for one week in Wyatt's life. And because, back then, days had faded one into another, Wyatt had agreed. By the end of the week, Wyatt had fallen in love with the work. And the purpose.

Both had finally stilled some of the restlessness inside him. It had shunned the aimlessness he hadn't known had been there until it had disappeared. He'd decided to try harder at university, though it hadn't been easy after three years of messing around. When Trevor had asked him if he'd wanted to study further, he'd wanted to say yes. But he'd known his academic record would prevent that from happening.

Except he hadn't known the power of the Bishop influence then. He'd been granted entry to an Honours programme because Trevor had, as he'd put it, 'put in a good word'. Wyatt had no doubt that word had come with a serious donation to the university. But by then, he'd been able to recognise that the universe had given him an opportunity. He'd taken it.

He'd passed his Honours with distinction. Had got into the Masters programme on his own merit. He'd felt good—but indebted. There'd always been that distance in his and Trevor's relationship because of it.

Some of the distance had been bridged after he'd started dating Summer. More so after they'd married. He'd asked Trevor for a lot of advice during that time. About having a family; being a provider, though heaven knew Summer didn't need him to provide anything. Occasionally, he'd ask about Summer. He'd rarely got answers he agreed with then. Now he recognised it as a sign of a strained relationship.

His caution with Trevor had remained even in those moments. For the first time, Wyatt wondered what it meant.

'She asked me for a favour,' Wyatt blurted out suddenly. He was so shocked that he wasn't offended at Trevor's own surprise.

'She did what?'

'A favour,' Wyatt repeated. It was too late for him to stop talking now. 'You said I'm doing more than cutting Summer slack, but it's because she asked me a favour.'

'Summer did?'

'Yes.'

'Are you sure?'

Wyatt's spine stiffened. 'Yes, sir.'

Trevor's gaze swept over Wyatt. He sighed. 'I'm not insulting you, Wyatt.' He paused. 'It's not like Summer to ask someone for a favour.'

Relaxing, Wyatt nodded. 'That's what I told her.'

'You told her that?' Trevor looked amused. 'What did she say?'

'She didn't like it.'

Trevor laughed. 'I don't imagine she did.' His smile faded after a moment. Wyatt watched with interest as Trevor's expression turned sad.

'Do you realise how much it must have taken from her to ask you for a favour?'

Wyatt stared straight ahead at the dining hall

of the lodge, which they were metres away from. 'I do.'

'Do you, really?'

'Yes,' Wyatt answered solemnly. 'I'm her ex-husband.'

'No, I didn't mean that.' Trevor stopped walking. Wyatt did, too. 'Summer is…careful with people. Not unlike you,' Trevor said, quite simply stunning Wyatt. But he didn't stop long enough for Wyatt to work through it.

'I admit some of that comes from having money and influence. People tend to want to be in your life for those reasons, and not for the ones that count. Summer picked that up right away. She was shrewd when it came to who she let into her life. After—' Trevor broke off. Cleared his throat. 'Years ago she became even more careful, which was how we knew you were the right man for her. She let you in,' Trevor said, 'and that was significant to us.'

Trevor let that sit, then continued, 'If she asked you for a favour, it's significant, too. Particularly *because* you're her ex-husband.'

Wyatt swallowed, uncomfortable with the direction the conversation had taken. But he knew that Trevor was right. Perhaps that was why he'd softened at her request. Not perhaps, he corrected himself. That *was* why. He'd agreed because her asking had told him she trusted him. And if she trusted him…

Well, as Trevor said. It was significant.

'No more of this, I'm afraid,' Trevor said suddenly, saving Wyatt from having to answer. 'Here they come.'

Seconds later, Lynette and Summer joined him and Trevor. Lynette's face was tense, her eyes sweeping over her husband's as if she were looking for something. Wyatt felt Trevor stiffen; saw him look at Summer. She shook her head and looked down. And then Lynette was hooking into Trevor's arm, squeezing Wyatt's bicep, and the older couple was walking ahead, though the easiness he'd always seen between them was gone. Both he and Summer stood, watching them.

'What just happened?' he asked.

Summer's expression was stoic. 'Nothing.'

He studied her. 'We should get back,' he said after a while.

'Yeah. Yes,' Summer said.

And then they were walking up in silence, too.

CHAPTER EIGHT

She'd known the conversation with her mother was coming. Had known it the moment her mother had made eye contact with her on that boat. *Might as well get it over with,* had been her philosophy when her mother had cornered her while she'd been speaking with Wyatt. Unfortunately, the conversation hadn't been as simple as the philosophy.

'Are you going to tell me how you've gone from not wanting to share a picnic basket with that man to sharing multiple intimate conversations with him? Not to mention a romantic boat cruise?' Lynette had asked shrewdly the moment they'd moved to a more private place.

'It wasn't romantic, Mother. There were thirty other people on that boat.'

'But there might as well have been none,' her mother replied. There was a pause. 'I take it your denial means no, you aren't going to tell me?'

'There's nothing to tell.'

'But he's upset you.'

The words were soft, concerned. Summer didn't respond. If she did, she'd have to talk about her marriage ending. Since her marriage ending had a lot to do with her husband trying to be like her father, she'd have to articulate why that was a problem. That would lead to the danger zone of her father's secret. Of keeping it.

No, it was best not to respond. Good thing she'd learnt that skill early on with the whole fiasco. Except that it had only added to the distant demeanour they'd already accused her of.

'Summer.'

'It's nothing, Mother.'

'Do not lie to me.'

Her throat thickened; her eyes burned. She didn't reply.

'Summer, darling...' Lynette sighed. 'When are you going to learn it's okay to confide in someone?'

A bark of laughter escaped from her lips. She almost covered her mouth from the surprise.

She cleared her throat. 'I'm sorry.'

Lynette sighed again. 'You can't keep running, my love.'

'I'm not running.'

'You are,' Lynette insisted gently. 'You have been for eight years.' Her mother's face suddenly became tight. She looked more her age than she ever had to Summer before. 'Your father and I hoped what happened... We hoped you wouldn't be affected like this.'

'Dad is concerned about this?' Summer asked, disbelief clear in her tone. 'Really?'

'Summer.'

This time her name was a warning.

'It's best if we don't talk about it,' Summer said, moving past her mother. A hand closed over her arm.

'You can't keep running.'

'But I have to!' Summer exclaimed. 'I can't talk about what happened. I have to keep running so I don't—'

She broke off, her heart beating hard in her chest. She took a breath.

'It'll be easier if you just let me go.'

She forced herself to look at her mother, whose expression was changing from confused to shrewd.

'You still love Wyatt.'

'What? *What?*' Her laughter didn't come as a surprise now. 'I do not.'

Ignoring her answer, her mother asked, 'Why did you end your marriage, Summer? And don't give me that nonsense about the two of you growing apart and focusing on your business,' Lynette said when Summer opened her mouth. 'Obviously that isn't true. Not after what I've witnessed this weekend.'

'You witnessed what we wanted you to witness,' Summer replied. 'We didn't want you and Dad to be distracted by our relationship during your anniversary weekend.'

Lynette studied her. 'You're lying,' she said with a perfect little scoff.

'I'm not.'

'You are. And you have been for—' Lynette broke off, her eyes widening. 'How have I not seen this?'

Summer nearly reached to her throat in an attempt to push her heart back down into her chest. Instead, she settled for that well-honed skill of not replying. It led to a long, awkward silence where her mother's eyes swept over Summer's face. She felt exposed by the searching, the studying. Felt as if her mother could see all the lies she'd been telling. The omissions she'd told herself weren't lies.

'Mom,' Summer said when the awkwardness became too much. 'We should go. They're going to miss you.'

'Okay,' Lynette said after a moment. 'Just answer me this.' She lifted her brows. Summer had no choice but to answer the unspoken question with a nod. 'Did you end your marriage because of your father's affair?'

Summer's tongue turned into lead. But the question was direct; there was no way she could pretend she hadn't understood. And heaven knew she was tired of lying.

'Wyatt admires Dad so much.' She spoke slowly, choosing her words carefully. 'He was turning into Dad. It made me feel...' She trailed off, unsure how to continue.

'Like me?' her mother asked.

'To some degree,' she allowed. 'More that he

made me feel like…me. In our family.' She swallowed. 'Part of why I married him was because he had a way of making me feel different from what I was used to. I felt…understood.'

'Because we haven't.' Her mother's eyes were compassionate. 'Not for a long time.'

'No.'

'What changed?'

'I told you, he—'

'What happened,' her mother interrupted, 'that he went from being the man who understood you to being like your father?'

Her lips parted, her tongue lifted, all preparing to give Lynette an answer. Except she didn't have one. She didn't know what had changed. She only knew that something had.

'I don't know,' she told her mother honestly.

Lynette put her arm around Summer's shoulders. 'Perhaps now's the time for you to get some answers.'

Summer took a breath. 'Maybe.'

'Definitely.' There was a pause. 'If I can do it, you can, too.'

'Do— What are you talking about?'

Lynette dropped her arm, brushing her skirt with the back of her hand. 'There's more to this situation with your father than I previously thought. Or I allowed myself to think about,' Lynette corrected. 'We're going to fix that before the ceremony tomorrow.'

'No,' Summer said, panicking. 'No, I didn't say anything—' She broke off. 'There's nothing... I was...upset. I didn't mean to—'

'Summer.' Lynette took Summer's hand. 'I've known something hasn't been right in this family for a long time. I know you've been hurting.' She squeezed. 'I knew it had something to do with your father's actions, too. But I've ignored it for eight years because I didn't want to relive the nightmare of the hurt I went through when I found out.'

Lynette exhaled slowly. 'That was selfish. I left you alone with your hurt for far too long. I hoped you'd get over it. Clearly, there's more to get over than I thought. I'm going to find out what I've missed.'

'Please,' Summer whispered after a long while. 'Please, tell Dad I didn't say anything.'

She had no idea why she said it. Why it was important enough for her to say it. But she was relieved when her mother agreed and kissed her forehead. They walked to the dining hall in silence, and found Wyatt and Trevor waiting.

When her mother didn't offer her father the usual affectionate greeting, Summer saw the confusion on his face. Her parents exchanged a look, and Trevor looked at Summer in question.

Did you tell your mother?

She shook her head, looked down. It felt like decades later that they walked ahead, and her body loosened in relief. Just in time for her to evade Wyatt's question about the awkward interaction.

'I suppose the polite thing to do is to pretend not to notice how tense you are,' Wyatt said as they made their way to the dining hall. He angled a look at her. 'You know, how tense you are about *nothing.*'

She laughed softly, too tired to fight off her first instinct. 'So of course you're going to ask me about it.'

'I didn't say I was going to be polite,' he said with a sly half-smile. It faded. 'Are you okay?'

She heaved a sigh, pulling the hat from her head and patting her hair. 'Yeah. It's just been a hard day.'

He frowned.

'What?'

'You…answered me.'

'Don't act so surprised, Montgomery,' she said, rolling her eyes. 'You asked me a question; I answered.' Then she realised what she'd said. 'I'm sorry. I didn't mean to call you that.'

'Don't be sorry,' he said softly. 'I didn't say I didn't like it.'

'Oh.'

There was a pause, and thankfully she didn't have to fill it when they reached the table. They were forced to sit in the only two vacant seats at the end. Her parents had wanted to sit next to one another at all meals, so they'd hired a long, rectangular table that extended wide enough in breadth for two seats to be at the end.

It was fine for them, since they were the anniversary couple. Though they probably regretted the decision now, she thought, taking in the tension between her parents. The seats were even more awkward for two ex-spouses. Especially after one spouse dropped a bomb on the other.

'I am surprised though,' Wyatt said after a moment, speaking quietly so that the guests closest to them wouldn't hear. 'You've been more cryptic this weekend than ever before.'

'And you thought I wouldn't be honest because of it?'

He gave her a look. 'The very definition of cryptic contradicts honesty.'

'I'm pretty sure cryptic means obscuring the truth. That's not the same as not being honest.'

'Isn't it?'

His eyes pierced through her. It was as if he knew about the conversation she'd had with her mother. As if he knew she'd realised keeping the truth from someone was the same as lying to them. But did he know that she'd kept something from *him*? Did he know about the affair? And how it had contributed to the end of their marriage?

For a second, she panicked. It took a long few minutes to realise she was overreacting. Her mind slowed down, giving her a moment to figure out what was happening.

When she'd asked for the divorce, she'd told Wyatt she needed to focus on her business. She hadn't mentioned that she'd much rather focus on their marriage. That she would have loved if he'd focus on it, too. But beyond asking her if she was sure, Wyatt hadn't done anything to indicate he wanted to fight for their marriage. In fact, he'd accepted the divorce so easily it was almost as if he'd...expected it.

Because of the pre-nuptial agreement he'd insisted on even though they'd eloped, things had been tied up fast. Just as quickly as Summer had found herself being a wife, she had been a divorcee.

'I don't think we should talk about this here,' she said quietly.

'No,' he agreed. 'Why talk about it here when you can postpone it till later and hope I forget?'

'I won't forget,' she promised. He looked at her. 'I haven't forgotten about the comment you made earlier about your parents.'

Wyatt's face immediately tensed. 'I didn't mean anything by that.'

'Now who's not being honest?' she asked lightly.

'Not fair.'

'I thought we already agreed things between us weren't fair?'

The waiter interrupted his answer by pouring them both a glass of champagne. Before he left, she got his attention.

'Sorry—is this non-alcoholic?'

'No, ma'am.'

'Could you bring us some?' she asked easily. 'Two glasses, please.'

'Of course.'

The waiter slipped away, and she looked back at Wyatt. There was gratitude in his eyes, but before he could say anything, one of her mother's friends, Pamela, who was sitting to their left, leaned over.

'No champagne for you, Summer?'

Summer smiled. 'Not today, no.'

'Any specific reason?'

'Like what?' she asked, frowning.

Pamela couldn't possibly know that she'd asked for non-alcoholic drinks because Wyatt's mother had been an alcoholic and he preferred not to drink. She hadn't wanted him to do it alone. It was always less conspicuous when two people weren't drinking, as opposed to one.

'Well, dear…'

Pamela's face turned knowing. After a few more minutes, Summer realised what she was talking about.

She burst out laughing.

'Oh, heavens *no*,' she said between peals of laughter. 'No, I'm not pregnant.'

'I don't see what's so funny about it.' The woman sniffed. 'You and Autumn are at that age where—'

Summer immediately stopped laughing. She had to stop herself from growling, too.

'I don't think that's appropriate to say,' Summer said with a stiff smile. 'Our childbearing abilities are no one's business but ours and the people we choose as our partners.'

Pamela blinked, her face splitting into a polite smile though her eyes were both embarrassed and annoyed.

'Of course, dear. You and Wyatt have seemed so close these last two days. And now both of you aren't drinking... I thought he wasn't drinking in solidarity.'

'Easy mistake to make,' Wyatt interjected, speaking for the first time. He sent her a look: *Let me handle this.* 'Summer and I made the decision not to drink when we were married, it's true. But since we've fallen into a friendship and the habit has stuck.'

There was a brief pause, during which Summer noticed they'd caught the attention of the couple sitting opposite Pamela. The Van Wyks were old school friends of her father's, who were apparently also interested in her childbearing state, taking their disappointed faces into account.

'I swear I saw you drink a glass of champagne at the picnic,' Mrs Van Wyk said with a shake of her head.

'Really?' Wyatt offered her his most charming smile. Summer was willing to believe anything he said next herself. 'Are you sure?'

'Oh, yes. She took the bottle—'

'You know,' Summer said, deliberately taking the baton in the imaginary relay race she and Wyatt were running. He had more to lose than she did. 'It's entirely possible that I *am* pregnant.'

She nudged Wyatt's shoulder with her own, trying not to laugh at the expression on his face. 'Friends sometimes do favours for other friends,' Summer added, winking at Pamela, since she'd asked the intrusive question in the first place. 'Anyway, we'll know in about two weeks. That's when I'm supposed to get my period.'

Summer made sure her face was perfectly pleasant and innocent, ignoring the shocked faces of her listeners. Saving them all from having to speak, the waiter arrived with two new champagne glasses, which he filled with the non-alcoholic champagne before removing the other glasses from the table.

Summer stood then, because, for the life of her, she wanted to make her mother feel good if only for that moment. It was a bonus that it meant the people around her would stop prying into things that were none of their business.

She picked up her fork, did the cliché tap on her now non-alcoholic glass of champagne, and prepared to give a toast.

She was amazing. Somehow, Summer had managed to put someone in their place politely, ensuring that they would never ask her—or anyone else, he bet—the dreaded *When are you having children?* question again. She'd also managed to refer to friends with benefits, sex, and her period while she did, all the while being perfectly respectful.

She absolutely deserved being called amazing.

He sat back as she clinked her glass, noting the way her fingers gripped the stem and knife tightly. It told him she didn't want to be giving a toast, and made him wonder why she was.

'Thank you, everyone,' Summer said with a smile that made her look as if she were a harmless little kitten.

Personally, he missed the claws.

'We're all here to celebrate my parents' anniversary. Thirty years together, no less.' She paused. 'Normally, I would leave this kind of thing to Autumn. Oh, don't pretend to be surprised by that,' she told the guests, and they laughed. 'We all know who the more charming sister is.'

Another wave of laughter went around the table, though Wyatt didn't see what was funny about it. He was perfectly charmed by Summer.

'But I couldn't let the second day of our celebration go by without at least saying on behalf of all of us—particularly from my sister and me—congratulations Mom and Dad. Your love for one another is beautiful.'

She looked directly at her parents. Though his gaze had been on her before, Wyatt now looked at Lynette and Trevor. Both of them looked more touched than such a toast should have warranted, though there was tension there, too. He couldn't explain any of it, yet Wyatt wasn't surprised.

'Here's to another thirty years.'

Summer lifted her glass, tilted it towards her parents, and sipped. Everyone at the table followed. Summer lowered back into her chair and let out a shaky breath. She immediately looked around, but the rest of the guests had turned their attention elsewhere. Except for him, of course, and she rolled her eyes when their gazes met.

'Glad that's over with.'

'So I see.' He angled his head. 'This is hard for you.'

She swallowed. 'Well,' she said with a strained smile, 'I wouldn't have minded some alcohol.'

'Why?' he asked, ignoring her comment. 'Why is this hard for you? I've never seen you struggle like this before.'

'I—I've never struggled like this before,' she admitted. 'At least not for other people to see.'

The sincerity, the pain in her eyes made him want to know more almost as much as he wanted to change the subject. Because he was keeping that as the question he wanted to ask her, he focused on the latter.

'Thank you,' he said sincerely. 'For doing what you did with the champagne. You didn't have to.'

She waved a hand. 'It's not like I'm a big drinker anyway.'

'You used to enjoy a glass of wine now and then, if I recall correctly. And—' he lowered his voice '—you did drink that champagne yesterday.'

She took her napkin and flapped it open, spreading it over her lap. It was another few seconds before she replied.

'I needed the courage yesterday,' she said, sending him a sly look.

His lips twitched, but he didn't smile. 'I don't think so. You're one of the bravest people I know.'

Her hands pressed against the napkin in her lap. 'I don't know what you're talking about.'

'You know exactly what I'm talking about. Starting a business outside of the Bishop name takes courage.'

'You can hardly call—'

'Standing up for someone when you don't have to takes courage.'

'You did it, too,' she said, brushing off his compliment. He wasn't surprised. She tended to do that. 'When you tried to save me from Pamela—' now her voice dropped '—and her inquisition.'

'I was offering you help because you were helping me out.'

'No, you weren't,' she said with a roll of her eyes. 'You were helping because that's what you do. You help people.'

He frowned, unable to reconcile that view of

himself with his own. When had he ever helped anyone else? His entire life had been about trying to help *himself* out of the situations his parents' decisions had got him into.

'Wyatt,' she said on an exhalation of air, 'from what you've told me...' She hesitated. 'Most of your childhood was trying to make sure you and your mother were okay. You helped her even though you shouldn't have been responsible for that. You shouldn't be surprised by that.'

Except that he *was* surprised. When he and Summer had still been together, they'd never had a conversation like this. The night he'd told her about his parents had been tense and quick. He'd said what he'd needed to say and that had been that. He hadn't given her the opportunity to ask any questions; she hadn't tried. Then they'd pretended it hadn't happened—at least, they'd never spoken about it again—and so of course he'd never heard her opinion about how he'd taken care of their family after his father had left.

And how he'd had to make sure no one had known about his mother's alcohol problem. His mother had made that clear.

'Keep our business private, Wyatt,' she'd said with that mean look she got on her face when she was drunk. 'As long as I'm alive, we'll be okay.'

Which, he supposed, had been the reason for his *help*. He'd made sure nothing happened at school to make anyone suspect his mother had a problem.

He hadn't invited friends over in case they'd see her drunk; he hadn't participated in after-school activities in case he got home and his mom had passed out. He'd been a star pupil at school, then he'd come home and made sure his mother kept breathing.

He'd done that for four years until he'd come home later than usual because of a compulsory school event. He'd found her passed out in her own vomit. That was when social services had become involved. After that, his mother had been in and out of rehab—had been sober and drunk almost as many times—and he'd been bounced back and forth between home and foster care.

How could Summer see *that* as helping?

His hand fisted on his knee. Moments later, Summer's hand curled over his, coaxing his fingers to relax. He looked down at it, then looked up into her eyes. They locked gazes, and he felt that tug in his chest. The one that told him she saw him. She understood. That was what had convinced him taking a chance on Summer would be worth it.

Look how that had turned out.

He broke the contact—of their gazes and their hands—and focused on the starter that had been placed in front of him.

'If it makes you feel less awkward,' she said, looking at her own food, 'you didn't help as much as you could have when we were married.'

'What?'

She offered him a smile he knew was meant to show him she was teasing. But her next words made that hard to believe.

'You were never home to help.'

He had no answer to that, so he left the conversation there. But all through his meal, he couldn't let it go. Then he remembered he didn't have to. He could ask her. Not now, he thought, nodding when the woman to his right offered him a smile when he looked up and directly into her gaze.

When she turned away, Wyatt leaned over to Summer and whispered into her ear.

'Do you want to take a walk on the beach after lunch?'

Her face angled towards him, confusion straining the beautiful lines of it, but she nodded.

'Sure.'

CHAPTER NINE

'MAYBE WE DIDN'T think this through,' Summer commented after they'd taken their shoes off, and were forced to put them back on when the sand burnt their feet.

That was what she'd been talking about when she'd said it, but she realised the words worked for agreeing to walk with Wyatt at all. Particularly when her control had slipped and she'd told Wyatt he'd never been home to help her.

She'd known something had happened while they'd been looking at each other, their hands touching. It was probably the reason she'd lost control. Then his expression had gone cautious. Which would have been fine. They were divorced, after all. But the problem was she recognised that expression from long before their divorce. He'd worn it throughout their short relationship.

So why did it sting so much now?

It was the universe telling her to turn around and run away from him, she thought. Except, as it always was with him, she'd lost her ability to listen to warning signs and logic. To try and protect herself. Knowing *that* should have had her not only running, but sprinting.

Instead, she was walking on the beach with him.

'If you don't mind walking in your shoes until we get to that cliff—' her gaze followed to where he was pointing '—there's shade over there.'

'Sure.' When it sounded too eager, she cleared her throat. 'I mean, I'm in if you are.'

He gave her a strange look but nodded...

And held out his hand as if it were the most natural thing in the world.

She took it, as if it were the most natural thing in the world.

Oh, no, the sane part of her mind groaned, reminding her of how awkwardly tense things had been between them during lunch. Pamela and the Van Wyks had given up on making conversation with them. Summer hadn't minded, but it had made the silence between her and Wyatt more awful. She wasn't sure where the silence had come from, or why, after it, he'd asked to walk on the beach with her.

Or why she'd agreed, and was now walking on the beach with him, holding his hand.

She angled her face up to the sun, hoping the heat of it would slide into her body and soothe the parts that were jumping up and down with protest posters in hand. Or perhaps she was hoping for a measure of the peace she'd felt earlier that day on the boat. Though she wasn't sure whether that had come from the sun, or from the fact that things between her and Wyatt had seemed less complicated then.

She almost snorted.

'What?' Wyatt asked from beside her.

'What what?'

The side of his mouth pulled up. 'You looked amused with yourself.'

'I am,' she said, grasping at the first appropriate thing she could think of as to why. 'I was thinking about what I did in there. With Pamela.'

The other side of his mouth curved up, too. 'It was spectacular.'

Summer laughed lightly. 'Don't be too impressed. I've had years of practice.'

'It did seem to have that experienced kind of flair,' he agreed. Now she did snort. They took a few more steps before he asked, 'Was it all innocent, though? Telling her off?'

'Sure.'

'Why don't I believe you?'

'Because you've never been polite enough to accept my answers at face value.' *Except our divorce.* The thought gave her pause, but she set it aside for later. 'There might have been a sincerer motive behind my impoliteness.'

'You weren't impolite.'

'I'm sure my mother will disagree with you once she hears of this,' she said dryly.

'And she will hear about it?'

'Almost certainly.' She glanced at him. 'You've been in these circles long enough to know nothing you say ever stays with the person you've said it to.'

His eyes met hers. 'That's not true.'

Her lips parted, and she slowly let the air release through them, as if she'd been deflated. She swallowed. Fortunately, she was saved from giving an answer when he asked, 'Are you worried about your biological clock?'

She blinked, then burst out laughing, just as she had with Pamela. *No.* She tilted her head. 'I've actually never given having children that much thought. I suppose it hasn't been one of my main priorities.'

'Hmm,' he said. 'I probably should have known that, considering I was your husband.'

She looked over. 'Do you want kids?'

'Not sure.' He gave her a dry look. 'I've never thought about it.'

She laughed. 'Oh, I see how it is. I'm a woman, so I must have spent all my time dreaming about the perfect wedding and the perfect family?'

'Didn't you?'

'My first—and only,' she added, 'wedding was arranged in the space of a week and happened in court. Does that sound like someone who imagined their wedding?' She didn't wait for an answer. 'There's no such thing as a perfect family.'

'Not even the Bishops?'

He'd asked the question deliberately, and something shifted inside her. She knew it because she hesitated—even though her instinct was to lie. From the moment she'd heard about his parents, Summer had recognised that thing pushing Wyatt to work as hard as he did was an idea. An illusion. He wanted the ideal life; the life he thought Trevor had. But there was no such thing as an ideal life. And for once, she wanted to be honest about it.

Even if she had to tarnish the illusion.

'Especially not the Bishops,' she answered.

Emotion tried to claw its way from her heart up to her throat. All of her bravado faded, and she changed the topic.

'That hasn't stopped Autumn from wanting one. A family,' she said, when her mind told her her transition might have been too abrupt for him to follow. 'A wedding. It's always been part of her life plan.' She paused. 'Maybe that's why she loves baking for weddings so much.'

They reached the shady section, and she kicked off her shoes before she let him help her sit down. Moments later, they were lying on their backs, their feet in the sun and the rest of their bodies in the shade, staring up at the blue sky. Something about it made her feel nostalgic.

'I remember Autumn used to make these scrapbooks of what she wanted her wedding to look like.' She dug her heels into the sand, then pushed her feet out before sliding them back together, bringing new sand into the holes she'd created. She repeated the motion. 'And she used to use literally anything she could find in the house and pretend it was a baby.'

She thought of the time Autumn had used a two-and-a-half-kilogram sugar packet as her baby, had punctured it by accident, then fallen asleep with the packet in her bed and woken up to ants.

Her *I'm a mommy* game had been confined to dolls and teddy bears after that.

'Anyway, she's been a bit more sensitive to things like what Pamela said after the whole thing with Hunter exploded in her face.'

She placed the back of her hand onto her forehead, letting the other one slide out next to her. On the opposite side of Wyatt. She didn't need any accidental touching. As it was, she was already struggling with him being close.

With him being close in that white shirt that made him so devastatingly handsome.

'I heard about their break-up.'

'I'm not surprised. Bishop Enterprises is a hotbed for gossip.'

'Actually, your father told me.'

'Oh.' Her feet stopped moving. 'Of course he did.'

'That's hard for you to hear?' he asked softly. She could tell that he was looking at her.

'No.'

'He hasn't ever told me anything about you, if that's what you're worried about,' Wyatt said stiffly.

Her head turned before she could stop it.

'I'm not. I wouldn't have cared if you'd known something about me,' she said, testing it out in her head to be sure. She was. 'Besides, he wouldn't have known anything I didn't want you to know anyway.'

'You would have kept something from him because of me?'

'No.'

She wanted to roll over so she could brush away the line between his brows. Instead, she looked back up to the sky. When the silence stayed for much longer than she was comfortable with, she went back to talking about Autumn.

Using her problems to avoid your own. Nice.

'The break-up wasn't easy on Autumn,' Summer said, when the thought made her feel nauseous. 'I thought I'd take one for the team.'

'You're a good sister,' he noted, though his voice sounded strange. 'I'm sure you told her she has more than enough time to have a perfect wedding and family.'

'I have.' She cleared her throat. His *good sister* comment had done something to her insides. Probably because she didn't believe she was a good sister. Good sisters didn't keep secrets.

'She doesn't believe me.' Summer frowned

slightly. 'It's hard to be somewhere other than where you thought you would be at a certain age. Especially for someone like Autumn. Her entire life's followed a plan.'

'Where did you think you'd be at your age?' he asked after a pause.

Her lips curved. 'Pretty much where I am right now.'

'Divorced?'

She grabbed a fistful of sand and threw it at his midriff, almost smiling when he twisted his body with a laugh.

'I was *kidding.*'

'Sure you were,' she said, giving him the stink eye. As he chuckled and brushed the sand off his shirt, she said, 'No, I did *not* imagine I'd be a divorcee at the age of twenty-eight.'

She hesitated briefly before settling on telling him the truth. 'Honestly? I thought I'd be somewhere in the management of Bishop Enterprises.'

He turned over onto his side, resting his head on his hand. 'Which is not where you are right now.'

'I'm in management,' she reminded him.

'Yeah, but it's not the family business.'

'No,' she agreed. 'It's not.'

His eyes searched her face. 'Why didn't you tell me you wanted to work for Bishop Enterprises?'

'I told you why last night. I thought it would mean more to build something for myself.' She took a breath. Answered his real question. 'It had nothing to do with you. And it wouldn't have changed things between us.'

He didn't reply.

'You more than anyone should know how important building is,' she said softly, turning to face him and mirroring his position. 'You've built an entire life for yourself. *By* yourself.'

He stared at her, then turned onto his back. Since she'd used the trick herself, she knew he was trying to avoid looking at her.

'Sometimes I find myself asking if that was worth anything.'

'What do you mean?'

'I've built and I've built but… I still don't have what I thought I would.'

Seeing the opportunity, she bit her lip. Sucked in air before diving in.

'Maybe… Maybe it's because what you thought you'd have wasn't realistic.'

He wanted to ask her what she meant, except that he already knew. At least in part. Having this conversation with her proved how unrealistic his wants were. And how he could never truly have what he wanted.

The opportunity to have these conversations with her whenever he wanted to. The pleasure of being the person she shared her thoughts and dreams with. The ability to listen to her laugh whenever he wanted to. To kiss her whenever he wanted to.

'It's not unrealistic because it's you,' Summer said, studying him. 'It's not realistic for anyone.'

'That's not true. It was realistic for your father.'

'No,' she said, her expression tight and pained. 'It's not. My father isn't—'

'It doesn't matter, Summer,' he interrupted.

'It *does* matter. This is part of what—' She broke off when he moved, staring incredulously when he stood. 'You're leaving?' she asked him. 'Wyatt, you're—'

Now she'd broken off because he'd lowered and scooped her into his arms, and was determinedly walking to the ocean. At least, that was what he wanted her to think…

'What are you doing?'

'Stopping you from talking,' he told her. He was rewarded with widened eyes and a curse so dirty he couldn't help but grin.

'I swear, if you throw me into the ocean, you will live to regret it.'

'I won't throw you into the ocean,' he assured her. 'I'll gently place you—'

She interrupted him with another curse.

'Wyatt,' she said through her teeth, 'please, for the love of all that is good in this world, put me down.'

He stopped abruptly and did as she asked, enjoying the surprise on her face.

She sniffed. 'Thank you. I assure you this was the best decision you could have made.'

'I'm not sure I agree with that,' he told her. 'But at least it gives you the opportunity to run.'

'To run? What does—?'

'Three—'

'Wyatt?' she asked, her eyes wide, which told him she'd finally comprehended what he'd meant. He didn't think she knew it, but she'd taken a step back.

'—two—'

'Wyatt Montgomery, don't you dare think this will scare me into—'

'One!'

She shrieked and began to run, and, with a grin, he followed.

Perhaps he would look back at this moment and wonder if he'd really wanted to avoid talking about his unrealistic dreams so much that he'd picked her up. Perhaps he'd wonder what had possessed him to put her back down and start chasing her. Or perhaps he'd just look back at this moment and see himself having fun for the first time in for ever.

Hell, he felt like a kid, running around freely, chasing someone he liked. Except he didn't know if that was true. He'd never had the opportunity to run around freely or play games when he'd been a kid. He'd been too busy taking care of his mother. Too busy being responsible and figuring out which steps he needed to take to get them a life she'd denounced as unrealistic.

Stability and security wouldn't have been real for him and his mother anyway. He'd tried hard during his teen years to get them there. To create a routine for them every time she left rehab. Even after her first few relapses and he'd begun to anticipate the moment he'd find her drunk again. Even after he would and he'd be forced back into foster care until she was sober again.

He tried again—and again and again—to turn their lives into something. He'd even thought he'd succeeded, when he'd turned eighteen. The routine had finally stuck. Things had been steadier. Weeks without drinking had turned into months, and he'd let himself believe it would be different this time.

He'd let himself believe it was safe to go off to university with the part-bursary, part-loan he'd taken out to live on campus and study. He'd returned to a 'For Sale' sign on the front lawn with his mother nowhere to be found.

He'd called the estate agent, who'd told him his mother had chosen to sell the very month he'd left for university. The house had been cleared out of everything, including his own things, and the agent had been in contact with his mother through a lawyer. When he'd called the lawyer, he'd got a bunch of nonsense about attorney/client privilege and he'd got the picture. His mother hadn't wanted him to contact her. She'd purposefully made it hard so he wouldn't.

He hadn't. He still didn't know where she was.

The experience should have taught him that, no matter how hard he tried, he'd never have the true stability and happiness he wanted: a family. People who cared for him unconditionally. Who wouldn't leave him.

Yet he'd still allowed himself to hope with Summer. He'd allowed himself to trust her. And just like his mother, Summer had shown him what a mistake hoping, trusting had been. So obviously, too. She'd been just like his father, pulling away from Wyatt first, then leaving. Because there were conditions to her love. She wanted someone who didn't come from a broken home. Someone who fitted her idea of the man she should be with.

He'd thought that idea was her father. When he'd sensed her pulling away, Wyatt had tried to be like Trevor. In some stupid way, he'd thought it would be enough to keep her from leaving.

Now he wondered if he'd got that wrong. And asked himself whether he'd ever learn.

He looked at her, running ahead of him, skirt flapping around her shapely legs, hair tumbling out of its confines at the nape of her neck. He pushed forward, enjoying her shriek, feeling it smooth something inside him even though he was sure she'd caused that something to crease.

Today wouldn't be the day he learnt anything.

He caught up to her easily, then ran a few metres ahead before turning to face her.

With a frown, she stopped, too, and said a little breathlessly, 'Aren't you supposed to do something once you catch me?'

'No.'

She tilted her head, waiting for more. But he got distracted by the curls that had escaped and were now wildly framing her face.

'Wyatt?' she said impatiently. 'Are you going to tell me why you've stopped playing a game you started?'

'Okay.' He frowned, trying to formulate a valid reason. 'It felt inappropriate.'

'What did?'

'Picking you up, then setting you down and chasing you.'

'What are you talking about?'

He sighed. 'I'm your ex-husband. What I just described could easily have been a plot to a horror movie.'

'You're my friend,' she corrected, 'and we were having fun.'

'Fun?' he repeated. 'You swearing at me and then running away was *fun*?'

'Well—yeah.' She pushed absently at the curls of hair that had bounced over her forehead. 'Weren't you having fun?'

His lips curved. 'Yeah, I was.'

'Okay.' She nodded, putting her hands on her waist. 'Okay. That's fine.' He wasn't sure who she was talking to. 'That's perfectly fine. We're allowed to have fun with one another.'

He smirked.

'Even if the fun came because you wanted to change the subject of a conversation we were having.'

His smirk died a swift death.

'I think we should get back. They'll start to wonder about us.'

'So let them wonder,' she replied, moving closer to him. 'You can't keep running, Wyatt.'

'I don't have to think about why you left if I keep running,' he said, the words slipping off his tongue. He couldn't bring himself to regret them.

Her expression tensed. 'My priorities changed.'

'Right after you found out about my parents,' he retorted, the anger he'd felt moments ago re-igniting.

Their eyes met. It felt as if a flare shot up and into the sky.

'Yes,' she said after what felt like an eternity. 'I found out about your parents and I realised that I would never be what you wanted.'

'You... No,' he said with a shake of his head. 'You realised I wouldn't be what *you* wanted.'

'What? No.' She paused. 'That's what you think?'

'You started pulling away from me after that.'

'Because I realised I wasn't what you wanted,

Wyatt,' she repeated. 'You told me about your parents and I realised all the work you were putting into your life… It was so you could have a life I could never give you.'

He shook his head, unable to speak.

'I don't blame you.'

'But you did,' he said automatically. 'You left.'

'Because the life you want doesn't exist,' she cried. 'I couldn't watch you strive for something that isn't real.'

'Why didn't you just tell me?'

Her eyes searched his face. 'You're angry. I'll tell you—'

'Summer,' he said, his voice low, 'why didn't you tell me?'

There was a long pause.

'It gave you purpose,' she told him softly. 'Before you met my father you didn't have that and your life then…' Her voice faded. She cleared her throat. 'I wasn't going to be responsible for pushing you back into a life that made you miserable.'

His mind raced at the new information. There was too much of it, and too many emotions accompanying it, and yet he knew she wasn't telling him everything.

'There's more.'

She lifted both her hands and placed them on either side of his face. 'Yes.'

'Tell me.'

'I can't.'

His jaw locked. But then her fingers moved, resting over the swell of it, lingering at where the muscles tensed, kneading them gently. Almost without realising it, he relaxed. Seconds later her hands lowered to his chest.

They were shaking.

'It was never because you weren't what I wanted,' she said in a voice that did the same. 'You silly man.'

He almost laughed. 'What was I supposed to think?'

'You were supposed to accept what I told you at face value.'

'That you were too busy for a marriage?'

She lifted a shoulder. 'You were,' she admitted. 'You were so busy trying to build your ideal life that you didn't have time for your wife.'

'Summer,' he said, his voice hoarse.

She didn't reply, and he lost his mind.

'I thought… It doesn't matter.' He shook his head. 'You were always going to leave. I just pushed you to do it sooner.'

Her eyes widened, before her face crumpled in emotion that broke his heart. Which made no sense. Her *actions* had broken his heart. Not her emotions. He stepped away from her when he couldn't make sense of it. Away from the heat of her hands, which felt as if it had seeped into his chest, reviving parts of him he'd thought had died when she'd left.

'You can't really believe that,' she said, folding her arms around herself. It made him angry, though heaven only knew why.

'It's the truth.' His voice was hard; it was the only way he'd get through it. 'Everyone leaves. My father left. Pulled away like you did before, too. Though thinking back now, I shouldn't have been surprised.' He took a breath. 'And my mother...'

He trailed off when his throat tightened. Besides, talking about her would only serve to upset him more.

'Those were the two people who were supposed to believe in me the most. And they gave up on me.' His eyes met hers. 'Maybe I could explain it by saying they didn't get to choose who I was. Maybe they didn't want me because they didn't like me.' He swallowed down the pain. 'But *you* chose me. You chose me, Summer, and then you left. Just like they did. Even though I tried—'

Suddenly his face was clasped between her hands again and she was staring at him intently.

'Don't you dare say I didn't believe in you, Wyatt Montgomery,' she said sternly. 'I did. I do.'

'But you still left.'

'So you wouldn't go back to the life you had before.'

'That wouldn't have happened.'

'It would have,' she said, eyes bright. 'If I'd stayed, I would have had to tell you...' She swallowed. 'It was the best thing for you, Wyatt. And it was because I believe in you.' She held his gaze. 'I would never give up on you.'

His heart felt as if it had been dipped into warm water after battle. He was stung, and bruised, and yet somehow still felt comforted.

'Okay.'

'Okay?' she asked. He nodded. She dropped her hands. 'This is so exhausting.' She blinked. 'Not you,' she said. 'Well, not entirely—' She broke off. 'I'm not making sense.'

'No.'

She let out a little huff of air, and her lips parted. For some inexplicable reason his eyes dipped to her throat as she swallowed.

His gaze lifted to meet hers. 'But that's okay. For now.'

She nodded, and the air between them changed. A pang went through his body as if it had recognised a piece of itself that had gone missing.

She edged closer to him. 'Really? Or are you just saying that?'

'No,' he said, and found it to be true. 'It's enough for now.'

'Okay.'

They stood like that for the longest time, looking at one another, barely any space between them…

And seeing each other for what he thought was the very first time.

So when she moved even closer to him, standing on her toes, bringing her lips a breath away from his, he answered by dipping his head to hers.

CHAPTER TEN

SHE'D BRACED FOR the contact, so much so that when their lips touched, she felt nothing—heard nothing—except for her heart pounding. She wondered if she'd see it beating in her chest if she looked down. Or if she'd be able to see it beat outside her chest since it felt exposed.

Then everything faded except for the feel of his lips on hers.

They were soft, tentative, and so wonderfully real. She felt the contact in her heart and down to her toes and, for some cliched reason, right to her soul. His lips began to move against hers and something sparked. Lust, desire. Whatever it was, it had her body sighing in relief. With pleasure. She had begun to worry the only thing this kiss would result in were emotions.

Then she felt as if she'd been plunged into the coldest depths of the ocean beside them. Her skin shot out in gooseflesh—each cell of it hyper-alert, hyper-sensitive—so that when his hands rested on her waist, she felt it throughout her body.

She paid no attention to the crashing of the waves next to them, or to the breeze that somehow both smelled and tasted like the ocean. She didn't think of the sun beating down on them, or how her toes were sinking into the sand.

No, there were only his lips on hers; his hands now roaming her skin; and the warmth of his tongue sliding against her own.

It felt as if she were a tourist in a different country, homesick and finally seeing someone from back home. It felt as if she'd been alone for years and were finally being reunited with her closest friends. And yet despite that, there was uncertainty. Caution. She didn't know whether it came from him or from her; either way, she was sure it came from curiosity.

Curiosity about whether anything had changed since they'd last kissed. About whether the emotions—the deep and raw feelings they'd shared with one another—would have any effect on the mating of their mouths.

When he moved closer, her body sighed *yes* and moulded itself to his. The uncertainty, caution, curiosity faded.

Her hands slid up, over his chest, and back down again, savouring the feel of his muscles beneath her fingers. When she'd seen him in that white shirt, she'd thought him handsome. It had hit her in the stomach, really, and she'd vaguely wondered what he'd have done if she'd gone into his arms before she could stop herself. Then she'd been distracted and she hadn't had to actively stop herself from being tempted by that face. By that body.

But she wasn't distracted any more.

She opened the buttons of his shirt at the middle of his torso, moaning when it gave her access to his skin. The moan came again when he deepened the kiss, and she was lost in the sensation of their tongues tangling and the pleasure and heat it had tumbling down her body.

They stayed like that for what felt like for ever. Kissing. Exploring. And though she knew her legs weren't working any more and that he was holding her up, she still kissed; she still explored.

Finally, they broke apart. And they stood there. Breathing.

Standing.

Until finally he said, 'Are you okay?'

Her heart, which up until that point had still been thumping in her chest, melted. His own emotions were likely up in the air about the kiss, but he was still asking whether she was okay.

That was the thing about Wyatt. He never did put himself first. He'd put his mother before himself when he'd been growing up. After his rebellious years at university, he'd put her father and the Bishop business first. For a brief—and, yes, wonderful—time, he'd put her first. Then, the idea. The illusion.

He was hurting himself by doing it. By putting himself second. His mother; her father; herself;

the idea… They were all unreliable. They weren't worth prioritising. Not even her.

Wyatt had already found that out with his mother. With her. If Summer told him about her father, Wyatt would realise it about Trevor, too. And the idea would unravel naturally, as he seemed to have linked it to her father…

Still, even after all they'd shared before that kiss, she couldn't bring herself to tell him the truth. Even after she'd repeated her mother's words to him about running, *she* was still running. From this. From hurting him.

Even if it meant hurting herself in the process.

She stepped back. 'I'm fine.'

'Are you sure?' he asked, his voice not giving away any of the emotion he must have been feeling.

'Perfect.' She cleared her throat when the word came out strangled. 'I'm just… I'm thinking about tonight. About the dance. The disco. Whatever.'

Oh, no, she was rambling. That never ended well.

But she was still talking.

'I don't particularly want to go. Not because of this,' she added quickly, 'but I… My parents… It's complicated.'

There was a long pause.

'So don't go.'

'Do you know who my mother is? She will find me and drag me to that disco.'

'What if I cover for you?' He stuffed his hands into his pockets.

'You—you'd do that for me?'

He lifted his shoulders.

'You don't have to, Wyatt.'

'I know.' His eyes met hers, which made her realise that he'd been avoiding looking at her since they'd stopped kissing. 'I want to.'

'You want to cover for me? Or you don't want me to go?'

She winced at the accusation in her tone.

'What do you want, Summer?' he asked, though the question was heavy and didn't at all feel as if he was asking about the dance. 'Do you want me to cover for you, or do you want to go?'

She studied him. And realised what he wanted her to say.

'Cover for me. Please. Thank you.'

She turned on her heel and left.

He'd offered to cover for Summer for his own selfish reasons. He knew it; she knew it. And she'd chosen to let him cover for her because of it.

It had taken him less than a minute to realise that after she left. It had taken more time to realise he had to come up with a reason why Summer wasn't at her parents' dance. And that he'd have to spend the dance mingling when that was the last thing he felt like doing.

But he couldn't bail, too, regardless of how

tempting the prospect was. He made his way down to the private beach that would be used for the dance. It was on the opposite side of the lodge to where his cabin was, and would be the venue for the vow renewal ceremony, too.

He shouldn't have been surprised when he walked into the large room, then. When he looked through glass doors out onto a patio that opened to the most idyllic stretch of beach he'd ever seen.

The patio and beach had been decorated for the evening's event. Colourful lights had been draped around pillars; both those supporting the patio, as well as the makeshift ones in the sand forming a dance floor. A bar stood to one side of the dance floor, lined with coconuts he assumed held alcohol. Considering the number of people on the dance floor who were swaying, holding their coconuts tightly, he was confident in that assumption.

The beach section was uncovered and open under the moonlight, which somehow made it romantic. He hadn't expected that. Or perhaps he was projecting how he'd felt the night before. When he and Summer had stood under the moonlight on that bridge, the sound of the ocean—

He stopped his thoughts in their tracks. He had to stop thinking about her like this. It was a mistake to indulge in fantasies about her. It had been a mistake to kiss her and discover that those fantasies had a foundation. Because she still wasn't telling him the whole truth.

Though what she had told him hadn't painted him in the best light. He'd made her feel as if *she* weren't what *he* wanted! He could still feel the shock vibrating through his body at hearing those words. But he understood them. Could see how the time he'd spent at work had led her to believe that work was more important.

What she didn't see was that he'd been working for her. Or he thought he had been. He'd wanted to give her the life he knew she deserved. If he couldn't be what she wanted, maybe he could give her what she wanted. What a stupid thought, he realised now. And he could have realised it earlier if he'd spent more time at home. If he'd paid more attention to his wife.

He'd been in his own head about how he thought she would respond to what he'd told her about his parents… He'd let it obscure how she really felt: that no matter what she did, she wouldn't be able to give him the life he wanted.

But it wasn't the life *he* wanted. It was the life *she* wanted…

Unless it wasn't?

'Wyatt?'

He turned, saw Lynette. Relief flooded through him when he realised he wouldn't have to think about it any more.

'What do you think?'

'Looks good. People are already enjoying it,' he said, nodding towards the dance floor.

Lynette smiled, though there was a tightness on her face that dimmed it. 'I think that has more to do with the alcohol that hasn't stopped flowing since yesterday.' She gestured to the bar. 'Can I get you something? We have many mocktails available. Or would you prefer something else?'

Wyatt smiled uneasily, wondering how she'd known about his non-alcoholic preferences. Had Summer told her?

'I don't have anything against mocktails.'

'Good,' Lynette said. 'I made a special request after lunch today. Which, according to my understanding, was quite interesting?'

His smile was more genuine this time. From relief, and that Summer's prediction that her mother would know about lunch had come true.

'Things always tend to be interesting with Summer around.'

Lynette tilted her head.

'Yes,' she eventually replied, quite slowly, 'our Summer does tend to make things more interesting.' She paused. 'I don't think I've seen her this evening. Have you?'

'I— No.' He cleared his throat, trying to remember what he'd come up with as an excuse for Summer not being around. 'She actually wasn't feeling well after our walk on the beach—'

'You two walked on the beach?'

Feeling heat push up his neck, Wyatt nodded. 'Yes, ma'am. We…had a talk.'

'People don't tend to have talks with their exes, you know,' she noted softly, her eyes both curious and…strained.

'I—'

'Nor do they sit next to one another on boat cruises. Or at lunches. Or ask favours.'

'Oh, leave him alone, Mother,' someone said from his side.

It took a moment for his brain to reset after it had scrambled with mortification. When he looked down and saw Summer, his mouth opened, just a little.

Summer looked amused. 'You've broken him,' she told her mother. 'Which means you likely gave him a much harder time than what I overheard.'

'Oh, there's been no hard time at all.' Lynette waved a hand. 'Has there, Wyatt?'

He shook his head, not trusting his voice.

'Anyway,' Lynette continued, 'how are you feeling?'

Summer frowned. 'Fine?'

'I…er…told your mother you weren't feeling great after the beach walk,' he jumped in, not wanting her to get caught in the web of lies.

Summer raised a brow at him, then looked to her mother. Her expression immediately changed. It took Wyatt a second to realise it was because Lynette's expression had, too. It had gone from easy, teasing to…strained, he thought again. Concerned even.

'I was tired,' Summer said, softly. 'But I had a nap. I'm feeling refreshed.'

If it hadn't been for her expression, he might have believed her. She was wearing a red dress that looked as if it had been made with summer nights in mind. It had cap sleeves that exposed the elegant curve of her clavicle and shoulders. Its neckline offered the slightest—though no less enticing—view of her cleavage; and it stopped mid-thigh, showing off shapely limbs that made him remember what it had felt like to have them wrapped around his waist.

Besides all of that, she was there, instead of in her cabin. She was with him, instead of far, far away.

Despite what he'd thought on the beach, he was glad for it.

'Well, darling,' Lynette said, her lips curving though Wyatt wouldn't call it a smile. 'I'm glad you could make it.'

'Is everything okay, Mom?' Summer asked, her own lips curving, mirroring her mother's not quite smile.

'Everything's fine.'

Lynette pulled Summer into a hug, pressed a kiss into her hair before patting Wyatt's shoulder as she walked away.

'For the second time today, I'm going to ask—what just happened?'

"I'm not sure,' she said, her expression pensive.

'I think…' She shook her head. 'It doesn't matter.' She smiled at him. 'What matters is that my mother just teased you.'

He winced. Lifted a hand to the back of his neck. 'I'm aware.'

'It's not a bad thing, Wyatt,' Summer said, her smile growing genuine. 'It means she sees you as family.'

He opened his mouth.

It stayed open.

Summer laughed. 'Almost a decade of creeping into her heart and you're still surprised?'

'I'm not family.'

'Not legally,' she agreed. 'Not any more. But you were invited to this weekend. And she's teasing you. Clearly she's realised there's no point in denying your relationship with the family is more personal than professional.'

'I'm not—it's still professional.'

She patted his shoulder, much as her mother had.

'If that makes you feel better. But my father wouldn't be grooming a man he didn't think of as family to take over the family business.' There was barely a beat before she said, 'Drink?'

She was already walking to the bar before his mind caught up.

Before his mind caught up, got distracted by the fact that she wasn't wearing shoes and that that somehow made her sexier, and then focused again.

'You're talking about this very nonchalantly,' he commented once he joined her at the bar.

'How am I supposed to talk about it?'

'I don't know.' He shrugged. 'I would think there'd be more emotion about your ex taking over your family's business. That he's seen as family.'

She ordered some tropical mocktail for herself, glanced over her shoulder for his order. He asked for the same.

'You've worked hard,' she said quietly, turning back to him. 'You deserve this.' There was a pause. 'And since it's not me, I'd rather it be you.'

He didn't have any time to process before she was moving on.

'Besides, my father's seen you as family long before our relationship. He's not going around offering internships to every bad-tempered university student.'

The barperson set down their drinks and she grabbed them both, offering his to him with a sly smile.

'I was not bad-tempered,' he said, choosing the most innocuous of what she'd said to focus on.

'You're right. I made it sound like it was in the past.'

He refused to smile at that. 'Did you come to this dance specifically to annoy me with perkiness?'

Her eyes narrowed. 'Don't you dare call me perky, Montgomery.'

He lifted his free hand in surrender, and suddenly realised the other patrons of the bar were staring at them, watching their interaction with unabashed interest.

'Want to find a place closer to the water to finish these at?'

Her eyebrows rose, but she turned, scanned the room before lifting her coconut. He followed her gaze and found Trevor and Lynette standing on the patio. Lynette responded in kind, but Trevor only nodded.

When Wyatt turned back to Summer, her eyes were tense. She covered it up with a smile.

'Sure. They've both seen me now, so I can abandon ship.'

He followed as she led the way past the dance floor, stopping right at the edge of where the waves crashed on the beach. She sat on a dry piece of sand, away from the view of the dance, extending her legs. He couldn't bring himself to care about the privacy she'd anticipated though when he couldn't stop staring at her legs.

It was fascinating, seeing the brown of her skin against the almost identical brown of the sand. He wanted to touch her legs; to take the sand and spread it over them to see how different they truly were.

Which was nonsensical, and more erotic than he should have allowed his thoughts to indulge. He drank deeply of the sweet drink in his coconut, relishing the burn of the sugar in his throat.

Perhaps it would burn away his insanity.

'Why did you come?' he asked, desperate to get out of his own thoughts.

She set her drink down. Began drawing circles around it in the sand.

'It didn't seem fair,' she said after a pause so long he'd thought she wouldn't respond, 'to force you into explaining my absence.'

'You weren't forcing me.'

'I would have been.' She carried on drawing circles. 'And now I'm forcing you to be here with me.'

'How are you forcing me when I asked you to come down to the beach with me?'

'Because...you don't put yourself first, Wyatt.'

'What?'

'You agree to share a blanket with me at a picnic because of my father. You agree to keep me company on the cruise because I asked you to.' She didn't look up. 'Were those really things you wanted to do? Or did you do them even though you'll regret them?'

'I didn't regret them,' he said after he'd processed what she was saying. And realised she was right.

'Not even that kiss?' she asked softly, abandoning her sand drawing.

'It was probably a mistake, but I don't regret it.'

She rolled her eyes. 'They're the same thing.'

'No, they're not. Regret is wishing you hadn't

done something. I don't—' he hesitated '—I don't feel that way.'

Her eyes were full of emotion he couldn't describe.

'And a mistake?' she asked, her voice husky.

'A mistake is…knowing you did something wrong.'

'So our kiss was wrong, but you don't regret doing it?'

'Exactly.'.

'Why not? Why don't you regret it?'

Up until that moment, he hadn't thought about the kiss. Or he'd tried not to, except to acknowledge that it had been a mistake and he couldn't repeat it. But not once had he wished he hadn't done it. Even now, when his mind told him it would be for the best to regret it, he couldn't bring himself to.

'I don't know, Summer,' he replied honestly. 'I guess it was nice to remind myself that our marriage wasn't a fluke. That there was a real, honest attraction between us before everything… Before.'

'You doubted it?'

He gave her a steady look. Her cheeks pinkened.

'Fair,' she said. 'But now you know the divorce wasn't because of that.'

'I still have questions.'

Her fingers curled into the sand beside her.

'So ask them.'

He hadn't expected that, but it didn't take long

to come up with a question. He'd been wondering it ever since their discussion.

'How could you have ever thought you weren't what I wanted?'

There was a long silence.

'Because you kept looking for more.'

'At work?' he asked. She nodded. He sighed. 'I wasn't looking. I was…hoping. If I could give you what I thought you wanted, maybe you wouldn't leave.'

She blinked. 'Why didn't you ask me what I want?' When he didn't reply, she said, 'The answer would have been simple: I wanted you. The man I fell in love with. The man you already were. Not who you were trying to be.'

My father.

He heard the words as clearly as if she'd said it.

It felt as if his heart had been torn out of his chest and lifted into space. It was too tight, too sluggish, too exposed. He waited for the feeling to pass, and when it didn't, he stood and began to pace.

'Wyatt—'

'I wanted to give you the life you deserved,' he interrupted.

'I didn't deserve you turning into my father,' she said so softly he might have missed it if he hadn't moved forward.

'You didn't deserve the instability I'd grown up with either,' he said through his teeth.

'Were those our only two options?'

'One of them wasn't as bad as the other.'

Abruptly he turned and walked towards the ocean. Almost immediately a wave washed over his feet. It happened again when he didn't move. And again, when still his feet remained rooted in the sand.

'Wyatt,' Summer said from behind him.

When he turned, she was standing a metre away from him. Gently, she took his hand and pulled him out of the water, closer to where they had been sitting.

'I'm sorry,' she said. 'I didn't mean to make you think about it.'

'No,' he said. 'It's not your fault. It's…always there. Hovering over my head. Work helps to keep it at bay.'

She dropped his hand. 'I didn't know.'

'I didn't want you to… I didn't want you to think I was broken. Or remind you I wasn't what you wanted.'

'I wouldn't have.'

'You wouldn't have,' he repeated, agreeing. Finally seeing. 'There's a reason I want that life you say is unrealistic, Sun,' he said softly. 'Realism wouldn't have got me out of my situation. I had to work towards something. My job… It allowed me to do that.'

Her eyes were wide, bright even under the night sky. She nodded.

'I thought,' he said after a moment, 'that I was working towards a good life for the both of us.' He looked down. 'I guess I was doing the opposite.'

'It's not your fault,' she said after a moment. 'I should have said something. I would have...'

She trailed off. He waited for more, but there was nothing, not for the longest time. Eventually, she said, 'This is my fault, too, Wyatt.'

'Why?'

'I—' She exhaled sharply. 'I can't tell you.'

He studied her. 'What am I supposed to do with that?'

'I don't know,' she said.

Her hand lifted, her fingers curling into a fist before it dropped. But then it lifted again, almost as if she couldn't help it, and cupped his cheek.

'I don't know.'

CHAPTER ELEVEN

FEAR PULSED INSIDE her chest.

She wanted to tell Wyatt the truth so badly, but that fear confirmed the only thing telling him would bring her was heartache. She felt torn between the two desires: tell him, or protect him. Or protect herself. The turmoil almost caused her physical pain.

A part of her suspected things would change soon anyway. Something had happened between her mother and her father. Summer could see it in the stiff way her mother held herself up; in the sharp glances her father sent her.

Even if Summer hadn't seen those signs, she would have known something was wrong based on her mother's behaviour. Lynette was acting strangely. Apologetically. And that could only mean her mother knew the truth.

So maybe she *could* tell Wyatt and finally get it off her chest.

But that wouldn't change the reasons she hadn't told him in the first place. She still wanted to protect him. She wanted him to keep his purpose. Except that felt up in the air now. Things had changed with him, too. They'd been honest with one another, and it hadn't destroyed him. It hadn't destroyed her either. Maybe she could—

The fear bounced inside her, demanded her attention. She dismissed the possibility. No, she needed to keep this a secret. And she'd just have to deal with Wyatt walking away from *her* this time...

Except he wasn't.

He should have. Her hand was cupping his face, and she was seeking comfort from him for her own selfish reasons. He should have been walking away from her.

He wasn't.

All she could think was that it felt good. Touching him felt good. Being there, practically alone in the dark with him, felt good.

She kept expecting him to push her away. To tell her that she didn't deserve to touch him, or feel good about anything that had to do with him. She held her breath, waiting for it. Waiting for the moment he'd realise he didn't have to stay there with her. The moment he'd realise his life would be so much easier if he left.

But it didn't come.

The longer she waited, the stronger the spell of the moment wove around them. The fact that the ocean was only steps away from their feet. The fact that the moon shone down over them, and the stars twinkled above them. Like the night before, when they'd met on that bridge.

Except it felt different now. As if the obstacles that had kept them from talking the night before had suddenly been overcome. Which they hadn't been, she knew, and yet it didn't change that things felt different.

Music drifted down towards them, mingling with the sound of the waves crashing in a seductive tune that made the spell impossible to bear.

Soon she wasn't thinking about what Wyatt should be doing. Or about what she should be doing. She was only thinking about her hand on his face. If she wanted to, she could slide it to the back of his head, apply pressure, and bring his lips down to hers...

It didn't help the fantasy—or delusion—when he turned his head to press a kiss into her palm. It seared her skin, so that when he tugged her hand away from his face, she looked down to check for a scar. She barely had a moment to see her hand before his fingers twined with hers. His free hand slid around her waist, pulling her gently towards him as he began to sway.

'Wh-what are you doing?' she asked.

'Dancing,' he replied, lifting a brow. 'Clearly I'm not doing it very well if you had to ask.'

'No, I—' She broke off when she realised how unsteady she sounded. 'I'm surprised.'

'That I'm dancing with you…at a dance?'

'That you're not running away from me.'

The light amusement on his face faded. 'If it helps, I'm wondering that same thing.'

'It does, actually. Not that I can tell you why.'

'Misery loves company,' he replied, the amusement creeping back into his voice.

'Loneliness, too,' she commented.

He looked down at her. 'You're lonely?'

She blinked when her eyes heated. Said, 'Yes,' before she could help it.

'But you have a family.'

'Doesn't mean you don't feel lonely,' she told him. 'Doesn't mean you feel like you belong.'

He searched her face. 'How did I get this so wrong? Your relationship with your family?'

'Is this your question?'

He blinked. 'What?'

'Your question. Your payment for keeping me company earlier.'

'Oh.' A puzzled look settled on his face, then his eyes sharpened. 'You'd like it to be, wouldn't you?'

'Just paying off a debt.'

He studied her. 'Fine. You've given me plenty of other questions. I suppose this one can be official.'

Something settled inside her.

'Well, then.' She cleared her throat. 'The answer is simple. You didn't know how I felt about my family because I hid it away from you.'

* * *

Wyatt stiffened. Her expression told him she'd felt it, but she continued as if neither of them had noticed anything.

'You know how, when you have someone coming over to your place for the first time, you make sure everything's in place?' she asked. 'You stuff the cupboard with your clothing, pack away the dishes, make sure all the surfaces are nice and tidy before they get there so you can impress them?'

He nodded, unsure of where she was going with it.

'That gives you a pretty good idea of what happened when I met you. Which is strange, because you were the only one who could see past what I was showing to the world.' She shook her head. 'The point is, I wanted you to see what you thought existed. Me, the perfect partner. My perfect family.' She paused. 'But I couldn't keep pretending like the clothing wasn't a jumble behind the cupboard doors. Or that I hadn't packed the dishes away into the wrong places, or that the surfaces stayed nice and tidy. What you've seen this weekend is…behind the pretence.'

'You're saying you stopped tidying up?'

She nodded. 'I'm sorry for it.' Her voice, her expression were sincere. 'I see now that I added to the idea of the life you wanted. But it's not real, Wyatt. I just pretended it was. At least, what you hadn't seen through.' She paused. 'I'm not perfect. Neither is my family.'

'Why? Why did you hide it?'

'Ah, that's a lot more complicated,' she said, her face sad. 'I've already told you some of it.'

'Purpose?' he asked. She nodded. 'We've already spoken about that. What's the rest?'

She shook her head, her face anguished, and he couldn't bring himself to ask it again.

He should have. Maybe he would finally get the answers he needed. Except he already had them. Some of them, at least. He saw that part of why she'd left had been because she believed she was doing the right thing for him. He couldn't blame her for it when he *had* needed a purpose. He'd needed something to work towards.

He didn't regret that desire when it had lifted him out of his broken childhood. But he could see how the idea of an even better life had ended his relationship. He'd had more than what he needed when he'd been married. Hell, he'd had everything he'd ever wanted. Still, he'd wanted more. He'd worked for more.

Not for Summer, he realised now. Summer had had the life he'd thought she deserved before she'd even met him. But he'd let his feelings about his parents cloud his vision. He'd let the brokenness they'd left inside him block his path.

And he'd hurt her because of it.

He should have been content with those answers.

He wasn't. He wanted to know everything that had contributed to the end of their marriage. He needed to know in case he didn't have to accept that he'd allowed his parents to rob him of his happiness.

But he couldn't ask her directly. Not when it had put that look on her face. So he hedged.

'For someone who doesn't feel like they belong to a family, you do a lot for them,' he remarked slowly.

'What do you mean?'

'Standing up for Autumn today. Making that toast.' He paused. 'Being here at all.'

'This is my parents' anniversary. I couldn't not be here. I tried, remember?'

'Summer, you can't deny you care about them.'

She shrugged. 'Caring about them doesn't mean I belong. In fact, it makes it clearer that I don't.'

'Did they do this to you? Did they make you feel this way?' he asked. 'I can't imagine Autumn or your mother—'

'Because it wasn't them,' she interrupted. 'Not intentionally.'

'So it's your father.'

'Wyatt,' she said, her voice low.

'It is.' He stared at her. 'Your father made you feel like you don't belong? How is that possible?'

'What do you mean?'

'How is it possible that he could make me feel a part of something bigger than myself, but he made you, his own daughter, feel this way?'

'Because you've put him on a pedestal,' she said darkly.

'He earned his way onto that pedestal,' he retorted. 'You know how much your father has done for me.'

'But he's human, Wyatt,' she said, stepping out of his embrace. 'Just make sure you have some steps for him to reach the ground. So he doesn't fall and hurt you both.'

'He won't,' Wyatt said stubbornly.

She snorted. Shook her head. 'One of the reasons I love you is because of your generosity. Your willingness to do things for people who don't deserve them. But this? This is— What?' she asked, interrupting herself. 'Why are you looking at me like that?'

He wasn't sure how he was looking at her, but it must have been some kind of combination between surprise and the warmth spreading through his veins.

'I—' He cleared his throat. 'You... Er...you said you love me.'

She frowned. 'No, I said—' She broke off, and all the colour drained from her skin. She shook her head slightly, then more vigorously as she took a step back.

'I obviously meant *loved*. Part of the reason I *loved* you is because of—' She waved a hand. 'It doesn't mean— *I* didn't mean—' She sucked in a breath. 'Look, tonight was a mistake. A mistake,' she repeated, 'not a regret. And I'm going to— I just need to—'

She turned away before she could form a coherent sentence. He stared after her as she walked, wondering if he should follow her and force them to talk about what had happened.

Except he could barely think it through. The uncertainty of it weighed down his legs, rooting him to the spot. So he kept watching, trying to figure out what the hell was going on between him and his ex-wife.

CHAPTER TWELVE

SUMMER COULD NOT fall asleep for the life of her. Which turned out to be handy, because when Autumn snuck in early Sunday morning, Summer was already awake.

'I told him I love him,' she said when the door to their cabin shut behind Autumn.

Her sister gave a shriek before a bump sounded. A few more joined that one before the lights went on.

'What the hell, Summer? Were you waiting up so you could scare me?'

'No,' she said defensively. 'I wasn't waiting up for you…per se. I couldn't sleep.'

'It's five in the morning!' Autumn interrupted in exclamation. 'The sun's coming up.'

As if hearing Autumn's words, the purple-blue sky began to turn orange.

'Is there a reason you're telling me these things?' Summer asked.

'You've been up all night?'

'Yes. Because last night I told Wyatt I love him.'

Autumn's eyes widened. She took off her jersey, kicked off her shoes, and curled up on the bed in front of Summer. She took Summer's hands in her own.

'What happened?'

'I don't know.' Summer tightened her grip. 'One moment we were dancing on the beach, the next I was saying "one of the reasons I love you". Not loved, Wind, *love*. Like, in the present or something.'

Autumn's face was carefully blank. 'Did you...? Did you just say you were dancing on the beach with your ex-husband?'

Summer pulled one of her hands out from Autumn's grip and put it on her forehead. 'Yes, but it was Mom and Dad's disco. Really, that's not the important part of what I told you.'

'It sounds important to me.'

'More important than the fact that I told him I *love* him?' Summer's voice was incredulous.

'Of equal importance,' Autumn replied, unfazed. 'The person I spoke to on Friday—or Saturday, for that matter—would not have danced with her ex-husband, let alone tell him she loved him. Love, sorry,' Autumn said when Summer opened her mouth. 'What happened to *that* Summer?'

'I don't know.' Now Summer stood and began pacing. 'I'd like to know, too. I'm freaking out.'

'Yeah, I can see that.'

Then Autumn stood, too, and took Summer's hands in hers again. Summer allowed it because that was their thing, holding hands. Something inside her eased.

'We'll figure it out, Sun,' Autumn said. 'But first, we're going to have a cup of tea because some of us got no sleep for normal, practical reasons. Like the fact that I've been driving for six hours through the night to get here in time for Mom and Dad's ceremony.'

'Which might not even be happening,' Summer said with a groan. She turned the armchair next to the bed so that it faced her sister before sinking down on it. And found Autumn staring at her.

'I'm sorry,' Autumn said. 'Did you say the ceremony might not happen?'

'Oh.' *Damn.* 'No. I'm sure it will.'

'Explain.'

'Mom and Dad had an argument yesterday,' Summer said, knowing Autumn wouldn't let it go if she didn't have some form of an answer. Summer would have preferred not to lie, but she'd been so caught up in her own drama that she'd forgotten herself.

'About what?'

'You know they don't tell me things like that.'

Autumn's eyes narrowed, but she began the motions of making tea. 'I take it there hasn't been a big reconciliation this weekend, then?'

'Sorry.'

Autumn didn't say anything, only finished making the tea. After she handed Summer a cup, she sat down on the bed and curled her feet under her again.

'It wouldn't be the end of the world if you put this behind you,' Autumn said softly.

'Except that I can't,' Summer replied sadly. 'Things are…different for me.'

'Why?'

She sighed. 'They just are.'

Autumn sighed now, too. 'Sun, you've let it affect so much of your life.'

Summer didn't reply.

'You were so afraid of being hurt that you divorced the man you love—'

'Excuse me?'

Autumn sipped her tea, eyes sharp on Summer's. 'Oh, I've forgotten what you said ended it? Your work?'

'I didn't want to hurt him by telling him about Dad,' Summer said tightly.

'You didn't want to *be* hurt by telling him about Dad.'

'You don't understand.'

Autumn studied her. 'I know I don't.' She paused. 'But Wyatt did, when you first got together. He understood you. Maybe you should trust that he will again.'

Summer's heart ached. She should have known that Autumn had seen through her. Especially after that conversation with her mother, when Lynette had admitted to knowing something was wrong with Summer, too. If Lynette knew, Autumn did, too.

It was worse that Autumn was right. Wyatt had understood her once. And she desperately wanted him to again. But…

'He'll hate me.'

'He won't.'

She looked down. 'Dad will.'

'Dad's an adult,' Autumn said softly. 'He can take responsibility for himself.'

She closed her eyes.

'Wyatt's an adult, too, Sun,' Autumn reminded her gently. 'Whatever his reaction is, he has to deal with it. Or you can do it together. But at least if you're honest with him, you won't have to keep wondering what would have happened if you'd told him. Maybe you'll finally be able to move past what happened with Dad, too.'

Summer didn't have the heart to tell her sister that that wouldn't happen. Not unless she could go back to eight years ago and change how everything had transpired.

But Summer smiled, and said, 'I'll think about it.'

'Okay.'

They sat in silence, drinking their tea. Eventually Autumn said, 'If you do still love him, and there's a chance you two can be together…' She trailed off, her face going sad. 'It's worth taking that chance.'

Summer knew Autumn was talking about her own relationship that had ended. She leaned forward and gripped her sister's hand. And though it was selfish, Summer thought it almost felt like before.

Wyatt didn't consider himself a fan of weddings. In fact, besides his own, he hadn't actually attended one. Which made sense. He hadn't made enough connections in life to be invited to weddings. No, invitations required friendships. Wyatt Montgomery had no friends.

Not even Summer, he thought, gritting his teeth. He'd thought they'd developed a truce of sorts. Then he realised that that didn't quite make sense, considering they hadn't been in a fight. She'd left, as he'd known she would. He'd accepted it, because he hadn't had a choice.

Except that didn't ring true any more, and he was too annoyed with himself—with her—to try and figure out why that was.

Instead, he made his way to Trevor's room, where his boss had asked to see him the night before when he'd said his goodbyes.

'Wyatt,' Trevor said when he opened the door. 'Come in.'

Wyatt walked past Trevor, his eyes widening slightly as he took in the large room. It was double the size of his own, with glass walls that offered a view of both the ocean and the steeps hills and mountains at the edge of the island. The interior was modern, with a touch of classic, its wooden floor panelling covered in parts with plush red carpeting, the walls decorated with antique African art and bright colourful paintings.

'It must have been a hardship for you to stay here,' Wyatt noted with a smile.

Trevor's mouth curved. 'Indeed. It almost made me regret picking this place to renew our vows at.'

Before Wyatt could ask why they'd chosen the place, Trevor's face fell. The older man walked to the decanter, put ice into two glasses. In one he poured sparkling water; the other whiskey. He handed Wyatt the water.

'I called you here for a reason, Wyatt,' Trevor said quietly. 'But I'm afraid that reason might no longer be relevant.'

'I'm not following?'

'I wanted you to be my best man.'

Wyatt wasn't sure how to reply. It was as if his brain had packed a suitcase, hitched a ride to the airport and was flying away. Far from where Wyatt could reach it to demand it give him something to say, apparently.

Anything to say, he thought, his skin growing clammy. His heart was thudding as the time went by and, still, he couldn't think of anything.

He opened and closed his mouth multiple times. A part of him was certain Trevor would retract his offer as he tried to figure out what was happening. Finally, his ability to speak returned.

'You said "wanted"?'

'Yes.' Trevor drained his drink, setting the empty glass on the table. 'The ceremony might not happen.'

'Why not?'

Trevor heaved a sighed. 'It's a long story.' His eyes narrowed as he looked at Wyatt. 'Summer hasn't told you?'

'Told me what?'

'She didn't, then,' Trevor said after a moment. 'I'm not sure if I should be content with that, or frustrated.'

'I... I don't know what you're talking about.'

'I'm sorry,' Trevor said. 'I thought—' He lowered himself into a nearby chair, looking older than Wyatt had ever seen him. 'Not sure why I thought it,' Trevor continued, almost as if to himself. 'She hasn't told anyone anything. Which is why things are such a mess.' He rubbed a hand over his face. 'No, things are a mess because I did what I did. I can't blame her for it. I shouldn't have asked her to do it in the first place.'

Wyatt wasn't sure what he should do. Trevor was clearly not speaking to him. And the things he was saying... They had nothing to do with Wyatt. They did have something to do with Summer though, which was why his feet were rooted to the spot. His curiosity, his concern didn't allow him to leave.

'I'm sorry,' Trevor said again. 'You shouldn't have to listen to my ramblings.'

Wyatt's spine straightened. 'Would you like me to leave?'

'No,' Trevor said immediately. 'No, I...' He let out a humourless laugh. 'Son, I don't know what I want.'

Wyatt's stomach curled into itself, then dropped to the bottom of his body. He swallowed. Breathed. But his head was swirling and his stomach was still in the vicinity of his shoes and he couldn't figure out what was happening.

'Lynette and I aren't on speaking terms right now,' Trevor said slowly. 'I'm not sure we will be by the time the ceremony rolls around.' He looked at his watch, laughed that sharp laugh again. 'In ninety minutes.' He paused. 'But I can't regret asking you, Wyatt. If there is a ceremony, I'd want you to be my best man.'

'I would be honoured.'

Trevor brightened for a beat, his face shining with approval. 'That means more than you could possibly know.'

'I could say the same thing,' Wyatt replied, though he wasn't sure he could. But he should have been able to.

Why did this interaction feel so...strange?

'You should go, Wyatt,' Trevor said, looking tired again. 'I'm not the best company at the moment.' He tried to muster what Wyatt assumed was a smile; he failed miserably. 'I'll let you know if things change.'

Wyatt nodded, leaving the room more confused than anything else. The one thing he was certain of was that he needed another shower. Sweat cleaved to his skin, making the one he'd had that morning feel as if it had been months ago.

He'd thought it a natural reaction to Trevor's question at first. He'd been put on the spot in an unfamiliar situation. But his skin still felt sticky, and his heart was still beating rapidly. And he could still hear Trevor calling him *son*. The term echoed in his mind as if it were a drop of water in an empty chamber.

His throat had begun to tighten at some point, too, and he was eager to get to his room so he could down a bottle of water. It would help with the tightness, he was sure. It would also protect him from dehydration because of all the sweating.

As he crossed the wooden bridge separating the two sides of the lodge, he saw two figures walking towards him. They were identical in height, and from this far there weren't many distinctions between them. Except his eyes immediately settled on the one on the left. His body's reaction to Trevor's question was timid compared to what it was doing now.

He swallowed. Did it again and again when that didn't take the tight feeling in his throat away. He forced air into his body with a deep breath, exhaling slowly before he was close enough for them to notice.

'Morning,' he offered when they were metres away from one another.

His eyes were still on Summer. She nodded, the colour on her cheeks deepening before she looked away. He dragged his gaze to Autumn.

'It's nice to see you again,' he told her, blinking when she walked up to him and brushed a kiss on his cheek.

'It's nice to see you, too, Wyatt,' Autumn said pleasantly.

'You were missed,' he said, when the silence extended long enough for him to think about Summer not looking at him. For him to realise he desperately wanted her to.

'You missed me?'

He smiled. 'That's not what I said.'

'No,' Autumn assured him, 'it's just what I heard.' She gave him a bright smile. 'I do enjoy hearing what I want to.'

'Autumn,' Summer said mutedly. 'Mom's waiting for us.' When he looked at her, she nodded again. 'Sorry, Wyatt. We have to go.'

'Of course,' he replied, embarrassingly grateful she'd said something to him. 'I'll see you there.' Then he remembered his conversation with Trevor and felt like a fool for not bringing it up earlier. 'Or you might not. I had a conversation with your dad that…'

He trailed off at the expression on Summer's face.

'Wyatt?' Autumn said in a tone that made him think it wasn't the first time she'd called his name. 'What happened with my father?'

'Summer knows.'

Summer was shaking her head before he could finish. 'I don't know anything.'

'Summer,' he said softly. His next words came from a place he had no idea existed inside him, but his gut told him she needed to hear them. 'It's time to stop running.'

Her eyes widened, became glossy. He ignored the frown Autumn sent him, and the way she looked from Summer to him and back.

'Be honest, Sun,' he said. 'Let them in. Let yourself belong.'

He nodded at her, then at Autumn, and walked back to his cabin. Once there, he stripped off his clothes and went straight to the shower, hoping the cool water would calm him. Or at least, help him think.

It had started with Trevor's question about Wyatt being his best man. Wyatt wished he could blame it on not having been in a wedding before. But this wasn't nerves. If it were, he'd feel calmer now. He'd only get nervous again when he was standing in front of the guests at the wedding. But he felt as if he was in some fresh new hell *now*. His skin felt as if it had been sunburnt—sensitive and prickly—and he still had to force his lungs to do their damn job.

But it had something to do with the wedding since that had started it all. It wasn't because he didn't want to be Trevor's best man. He did. Not because he felt indebted, but because…he wanted to.

He saw now that it hadn't been a lie when he'd said it meant something for Trevor to ask. It took him a moment, but he realised that admission changed his relationship with Trevor. He didn't know what had changed; only that something had.

And *that* was what felt strange. The fact that Trevor had asked at all. That he had called Wyatt *son*. Wyatt had thought about weddings and connections before, but what did this mean? If attending a wedding simply meant having a connection, what did being in one mean? What was deeper than having a connection with someone?

Family.

Summer had told him her parents considered him family the night before. It had been unsettling hearing it then, but he only now figured out why.

He didn't know how to be family. He'd never had one. Certainly not one like the Bishops. Though he didn't really know what that meant now. He'd idealised their family; Summer had made that clear. And he'd seen it himself.

But they were still more of a family than he'd ever had. His only example of familial relationships had been his parents' abandonment. His first and only attempt at creating his own family with Summer had failed.

Why did thinking about that make his heart ache? Why did it make fear thrum in his veins?

He didn't know. But as he got out of the shower, Wyatt was determined not to think about it.

CHAPTER THIRTEEN

EVEN IF WYATT hadn't warned her, Summer would have known something was wrong the moment she walked into the room.

The lodge had prepared a room for Lynette to get ready in, but it looked as if it had been used for more than that. The bed was unmade; her mother's suitcases were in the corner. Lynette was sitting in a white nightgown on a chair, staring into the cup in her lap. Summer couldn't tell if anything was inside it.

'Mom,' Autumn said after taking everything in. 'Are you okay?'

Lynette's eyes lifted lethargically, as if she hadn't realised they'd walked into the room. Her expression softened when she saw Autumn.

'Honey, I didn't know you were here.'

'Of course I'm here,' Autumn said, sitting on the chair next to her mother. 'You and Dad are renewing your vows.'

Lynette looked down again, but not before Summer saw her mother's eyes fill. She stood, unmoving, before lifting her shoulders when Autumn shot her a look. *Help,* it screamed. But how could she help when this was her fault?

'I'm not sure we'll be doing that, Autumn.' Her mother's voice was soft but firm. 'Your father and I are…not on the same page any more.'

'What does that mean?'

Lynette's head lifted, and she looked directly at Summer. 'Why didn't you tell me, darling?'

Her legs began to shake, though Summer couldn't be sure that hadn't started the moment she'd seen Wyatt. If not then, surely when he'd told her to be honest. To let herself belong. She'd been hopeful in that moment, thinking about the possibility of belonging again. But she was sure now it wouldn't happen. Keeping her father's secret had already brought such destruction. How could being honest be any different?

The look on her mother's face told her she no longer had a choice though.

She took a deep breath. 'He asked me not to.'

'And you listened to him?' Lynette asked. 'I raised you better than that.'

'But the man who raised me alongside you asked me to do this. It wasn't…' She blew out a breath. 'This wasn't a failing in how you raised me, Mom. It wasn't my moral decision. This wasn't my decision at all.'

'That,' Lynette said, her fingers tightening on her mug, 'is not true.'

'Okay,' Autumn said into the tight quiet that

followed their mother's words. 'Clearly I'm missing something here.' She looked from Lynette to
Summer. 'Care to explain?'

'I knew about the affair,' Summer said, tired
of the secret now. 'I found out before the O'Brien
deal went through. Dad asked me not to tell you
and Mom until the papers were signed.'

'What?'

Summer didn't answer. Instead, she walked
onto the patio, resting her forearms on the bal-
cony railing. She took a deep breath, letting the
sea air soothe her. Except it reminded her of Wyatt
now. Of when he'd chased her along the edge of
the water. Of when they'd kissed. Of when they'd
danced.

Let yourself belong.

She walked back into the room.

'Sun,' Autumn said as soon as she did, 'how
long did you know?'

'Two months,' she answered. Inhaled. Exhaled.
'That's when I started separating myself from the
family. I wanted to tell you both so badly. I didn't
want to be alone in it. I know that sounds selfish—'

'It doesn't,' her sister interrupted. 'Part of why
I could get through it was because I wasn't doing
it alone. We all were. At least, I thought so,' she
added, pained.

'No, you didn't think that,' Summer said. 'You
knew I was struggling. You both did.' She paused.
'And this is why, by the way. Not because I was

clinging to the past, or because I couldn't get over Dad breaking our trust—'

She stopped at that. Took a moment to figure out why it felt significant. She'd spent so much time resenting him for asking her to keep the affair a secret that she hadn't truly thought about the affair itself.

No, that wasn't true, she thought immediately. She had thought about it. And she had felt betrayed—about both things. Her father cheating on her mother *and* asking her to keep it a secret.

She shook her head. She'd think about it later.

'I couldn't forgive him for breaking up our family,' she continued quietly. 'Not only because of his affair, but because of what it did to me in our family. It…pushed me out.'

Both Autumn and Lynette moved towards her, but Autumn fell back and let Lynette pull Summer into a hug. Summer heard the sob that came from her mouth as if it were in the distance, but she managed to stop any more from escaping. She didn't want to break open now. She still wasn't sure what would spill out.

But she clung to her mother, needing the comfort. Feeling, for the first time in for ever, as if Lynette finally understood.

Lynette pulled back. 'I'm sorry you went through that.'

'Thank you,' she said, sincerity coating her words.

'I wish you'd told me.' Lynette brushed Summer's hair away from her face. 'Then we wouldn't be here.'

'Wouldn't we?' Summer asked.

'No,' Lynette said decisively. She went back to her seat, lowering down regally. 'I wouldn't have said yes to your father's proposal if I'd known.'

'Dad proposed?' Summer tilted her head. 'Why didn't I know that?'

Lynette lifted a shoulder. Something jiggled inside Summer's chest.

'Anyway,' Summer said, ignoring it, 'you know you would have said yes, Mom.'

'No, I—'

'This isn't worse than him cheating on you.'

Lynette's face tightened. 'So you say.'

'Because I know,' Summer said. 'I know you and Dad. If you could work through the affair, you can work through this.' She paused. 'There was no real damage, Mother.'

'You must be joking,' Lynette said, straightening. 'You've spent the last eight years in pain. And your father knew it. He did nothing about it.' She pressed a hand to her stomach. 'You should never have felt like an outsider to this family, Summer.'

'But that was just as much me as it was Dad,' she said, realising its truth. She swallowed. 'I think Dad did a cost benefit analysis and realised he'd rather hurt me than you.' She took an unsteady breath. 'Which would have happened if he'd told you the truth, clearly.' She paused. 'I understand why he did it.'

'I don't,' Lynette said stubbornly.

Summer looked at Autumn then, tilting her head towards their mother.

Autumn lifted her brows. *Are you sure?* she was asking. Summer nodded. When Autumn wordlessly asked why, Summer shrugged.

She didn't know why she wanted to make things right. Maybe she was tired of a broken family. Now that Autumn and her mother knew the truth, she wouldn't have to hide anything any more. They could move forward. She could belong.

She wasn't sure she could tie this up so simply, particularly when she hadn't even thought about where her father fitted into all of it. But she didn't want her mother to hurt. Not for her sake, anyway. Not when her mother was right: she'd made a choice to keep the truth from them. By doing so, she'd continued to play the outsider role. She'd had a say in that, too.

She couldn't quite wrap her head around it though, so she pushed it aside. Pushed the emotions down, too.

'I think Summer's right,' Autumn said, on cue. 'You've spent the last eight years working through this. You've built a marriage that's stronger.'

'And yet I still can't trust him.'

'Of course you can,' Summer said, waving a hand. 'Dad's changed in the last eight years.' She frowned. 'More than I realised.' She shook her head. 'He's put you first since then, Mom. Wyatt has more responsibility at Bishop Enterprises now because Dad's spent more time at home. With you. Working on rebuilding that trust. Your marriage is important to him.'

Defending her father felt strange, but the words weren't lies. She still didn't know what to do about that knowledge.

'What happened with me... He was wrong, Mom, but I don't think he was trying to hide it from you. He just didn't want to jeopardise what you've worked so hard to rebuild.'

Silence followed Summer's words. She held her breath, trying to anticipate her mother's next argument.

'It ruined your marriage, Summer,' Lynette said. Summer certainly hadn't anticipated that. 'You clearly still love Wyatt. The reason you two divorced isn't because of your work, like you told us.'

'No,' Summer agreed, speaking over the lump in her throat. 'It's because I...was afraid of being hurt like you were,' she said, grasping the reason Autumn had given her that morning. She leaned more heavily on the crutch. 'I was afraid to trust someone again.' She sucked in air. 'But I'm an adult, Mom. It was my choice. It's my responsibility. I've accepted that.'

'What about—?'

'No,' Autumn interrupted. 'Now you're just

looking for an excuse to get out of this.' Autumn took Lynette's hands, drew her up. 'I think you're getting cold feet.'

'I am *not*.'

'Great.' Autumn grinned. 'You have no more reason to delay this wedding.' Autumn looked at her watch. 'With thirty minutes to spare, too.' She paused. 'Can I tell Dad you've forgiven him?'

Lynette's eyes swept over Summer. Summer nodded, giving her the most genuine smile she could manage. When her mother's face brightened, Summer thought she deserved a prize for acting.

'Tell him the ceremony will continue,' Lynette said. 'Don't let him know I forgive him yet.' She sniffed. 'He can spend some more time being miserable. It can be his penance for doing what he did to Summer.'

Summer's smile came more naturally now.

CHAPTER FOURTEEN

HER MIND WAS still a mess by the time they made their way down to the beach for the ceremony. Fortunately, Autumn was walking in front with Lynette, chatting about nothing in particular. Summer knew her sister was doing so purposefully. Autumn had sent her shrewd looks the entire time they'd spent getting ready; she knew how much Summer had borrowed from their conversation to make their mother feel better.

If they both hadn't been determined to get Lynette down the aisle, Summer was sure Autumn would have said something. But they were, thankfully. And Autumn was nothing if not a team player, so the chattering's intention was to keep Lynette from noticing Summer's silence.

It was a relief when they finally reached the beach. It was the same venue as where the disco had been the night before. This time, the inner venue had been transformed into a dining hall. Three long tables were arranged at an angle in the room, with one smaller table on one end.

All the tables were decorated with white cloths and yellow runners. A bright, bold flower arrangement stood at each end; tea-light candles had been placed on top of white petals running between the arrangements. The smaller table had 'Mr and Mrs, Again' carved in wood at its front. Fairy lights hung down the wall behind the table.

The patio was void of any lights, and had been softened with vases and pots of white, yellow, and pink flowers. A carpet extended from the sliding doors of the venue down, over the patio to the front of where Summer assumed her parents would be renewing their vows. She had to assume as her view of that area was currently obscured by a large arch of greenery and white, yellow, and pink flowers that had been placed at the beginning of the beach.

'Wow,' Summer breathed. 'This is... Wow.'

'Thank you.' Lynette smiled thinly. She'd recovered enough to be nervous. 'Your sister and I have been working on this for months.'

Lynette put an arm around Autumn and squeezed. Something inside Summer squeezed, too.

'You've been helping with this?' she asked Autumn. 'Why didn't either of you tell me? Or ask me to help?'

Lynette and Autumn exchanged a look.

'We thought you wouldn't be interested, dear,' Lynette said. She took a step forward, brushing a curl from Summer's forehead. 'But you're here. And we're a family again. That's enough.'

She kissed Summer's head and took a deep breath. The show of nerves made Summer realise now wasn't the time for her emotions. She could be offended at how low the bar was later. She could think about her mother being pleased that she'd simply *attended* a family event later. She wouldn't think about how it showed how much of an outsider she'd allowed herself to become now.

No, now, she'd offer her mother a smile.

'You look breathtaking, Mom. Dad isn't going to know what hit him.'

Her mother smoothed down the front of the simple white dress she wore. It had sleeves and lowered into a modest V at her neck. There was a yellow belt at its waist; the rest of the white material fell down to her bare feet. Her curls were tamed into a bun, though some strands of them had escaped and sprung around the yellow flower Summer had tied in her hair minutes ago.

For some reason, the picture of it had Summer blinking back tears. She forced her smile wider instead. Autumn gripped her hand, squeezed. Then it was time for them to walk down the aisle.

Summer had never been more grateful for the beach than at that moment. The wind was blowing lightly, and the sun wasn't strong enough to do anything other than tenderly warm the earth.

She took a deep breath of salty fresh air and followed Autumn down the aisle.

The first thing she saw was the white arch at

the end of the aisle. It had been made of wire, and had greenery and flowers curving around it like the first arch. The second thing she looked at was her father. He looked...grateful, she thought. When her mother started the walk down the aisle, Summer watched him blink back tears.

It felt like proof her father had changed. Or become a better version of himself. A combination of the good things of the man she'd thought she'd lost all those years ago and someone who was trying. That last part made a difference, she thought. Trevor had always been a good man. His priorities had been skewed, and that had led him down a dark path. But he'd changed those priorities. He was trying to put his family first this time. And he'd succeeded... With Autumn and Lynette.

It still stung that he hadn't tried with her.

She believed everything she'd told her mother. She knew her father had weighed up hurting his wife against hurting his daughter. His daughter had lost. Which, she supposed, was to be expected. She couldn't even blame him for it.

What she did blame him for was teaching Wyatt to do the same thing.

It was my choice. It's my responsibility.

The memory of her words forced Summer into remembering she'd contributed to the end of her relationship, too. Hell, she'd just realised she'd contributed to isolating herself from her family as well. There were myriad examples of times when she'd excluded herself. Enough that her mother hadn't even asked her to help plan the vow renewal.

She'd told herself her father had broken their family. And that Wyatt's actions had ended their marriage. She'd conveniently removed her own culpability in the process.

Watching Summer walk down the aisle had given him chills.

The chills hadn't been the bad kind. They hadn't been because he'd been frightened by seeing his ex-wife walk down the aisle. Seeing her hadn't caused his stomach to turn. It hadn't caused nausea, nor the hundreds of other reactions he should have had at seeing a woman he'd divorced walk down an aisle again.

No, his chills had been of the good kind. They'd accompanied the thought that he'd lost out by suggesting they marry in court. And *that* thought had been accompanied by a longing he'd felt so rarely in his life he could count the instances on one hand.

Like the time he'd seen a father and son having a meal together in a restaurant when he'd been sixteen. Or when he'd been twenty-four and he'd seen a man and his mother reunite at the airport.

The longing always—*always*—came with regret. He didn't care for it.

So Wyatt desperately tried to ignore Summer altogether. He was determined not to think about her standing on the opposite side of the aisle. It should have been easier than it was considering she barely looked at him. He knew that because his efforts were failing. He tried to focus on the ceremony again.

Again, he did not succeed.

His eyes slid over to her and he thought that, perhaps, he was being too hard on himself. Almost everyone else in attendance must have felt the same way. The Bishop sisters made a startling picture as the maids of honour—titles Trevor had informed him of with great amusement.

Though Trevor's smile could have come from his relief that the ceremony was on again.

Both sisters were dressed in yellow. Autumn's dress was a bright shade that looked as if it had been made for a summer wedding; Summer's a much lighter colour. The styles of their dresses were also different, though this time Autumn's seemed demurer and Summer's more audacious. It was intricately designed, so naturally he couldn't describe it. All he knew was that he could see a leg and an arm and he felt lucky for it.

Then there was her hair.

She wore it in one big mass of curls around her head, accentuated by a large yellow flower, slightly smaller than the one that had been pinned to Lynette's hair. He was sure Summer had teased those curls so that they looked bigger and bolder than what he'd seen before. It was the first time this weekend he'd seen her hair loose, too, and his fingers itched to pull at the curls.

Her face went from tortured to carefully blank, as if she'd realised people were watching her. He still saw the torture reflected in her eyes though. He wondered what could possibly have happened in her relationship with her father to put that hurt there.

He was so deep in thought about it that he missed his cue to hand Trevor the rings. He frowned when he caught Summer looking at him. It took him an embarrassingly long time to realise Summer wasn't the only one.

'Sorry,' he mumbled, handing Trevor the rings.

Trevor chuckled, winking at Wyatt as he took them. Wyatt purposefully avoided looking at Summer after that. Before he knew it, Trevor and Lynette were sharing a kiss.

Almost immediately after, the guests were told to relax while photos were taken. He followed the guests until Trevor called him to be a part of the photos. Somehow he hadn't realised that was part of the best man duties. After an inordinate amount of smiling, he was back to being grateful he and Summer had decided on a court wedding.

Summer looked as if she were grateful for that fact, too.

When they were finally given permission to leave so Lynette and Trevor could take solo photos, Summer turned on her heel and walked off. They all watched, though it was Trevor Wyatt glanced at shortly after. The man's gaze was pinned to Summer's retreating figure, before he exchanged a look with Lynette.

'She's fine,' Autumn said brightly at his side. Wyatt opened his mouth to contradict her, but was silenced with one look. 'Go ahead, Mom and Dad. Enjoy.'

She waited until her parents were gone, then turned to Wyatt.

'Shouldn't you go after her?' he asked after an awkward silence.

Autumn's expression turned pensive. 'No,' she replied. 'No, I don't think she needs me right now.'

'Who else is there?'

Autumn lifted a brow. It took a thudding heart to realise she was talking about him.

'Oh.' He paused. 'No.'

'No?'

'She's not my responsibility.'

It felt like an excuse.

It felt like a lie.

'Not legally, no,' Autumn said. 'But apparently things have happened between you two this weekend?'

'Not things that make going after her my responsibility.'

'Really?' she asked dryly. 'Dancing on the beach doesn't carry emotional strings for you, then?'

His face grew warm, and he rubbed a hand along

the back of his neck. 'I didn't realise you knew about that.'

'That you're a romantic?'

'I'm not—'

He broke off when he realised she was teasing him. Besides, it did sound romantic.

Did Summer think so too?

'Anyway,' he said, deliberately changing the topic, 'I don't think she wants me.'

'Maybe not.' Autumn's face softened. 'But I think she needs you.'

He wanted to ask her what she meant, but she squeezed his arm and walked away.

He stared after her. When she didn't turn back, Wyatt sighed and went in search of his ex-wife.

CHAPTER FIFTEEN

SUMMER WATCHED THE waves crash against the rocks that created the natural boundary of the private beach where the ceremony had been held. It made her feel trapped. For a minute, she fantasised about climbing over the rocks to escape the feeling. Surely being able to breathe properly would be worth her dress? Her hair? Her make-up?

Another part of her wanted to walk into the ocean. To feel the cool water flow over her skin that suddenly felt too hot. To feel the waves carry some of the weight that was pressing on her shoulders, her chest. To have the salt burn her eyes instead of the tears.

She knew leaving as soon as she could would probably worry her mother. And her sister. But Summer couldn't stay there with her too-hot skin and her weighed-down shoulders and chest. She sure as hell couldn't stay there when it felt as though the tears would fall down her cheeks at any moment.

But crying felt like an admission. Instead of giving in to the temptation, Summer closed her eyes and pressed a hand to that spot just beneath her breasts that expanded with air. She let herself breathe. Let herself feel the air move in and out of her lungs. It helped her feel steadier, until she felt the air shift around her. She opened her eyes and found herself looking directly into Wyatt's.

'How long have you been there?' she asked unsteadily.

'Not long.'

He put his hands in the black trousers he wore. They were rolled up at the ankles, revealing his bare feet. They looked out of place with his white shirt and yellow bow-tie. But the whole thing reminded her of how cute he'd looked when she'd first seen him. As soon as she'd thought it, the demons of regret kidnapped her thoughts.

'I see you were forced to participate in this, too.'

'Not forced,' he disagreed.

She nodded. Took another breath. 'Why are you here?'

'You're upset.'

'I am,' she said, ignoring the tightening of her throat at how vulnerable admitting it made her feel. 'But it isn't your responsibility to come after me.'

'Autumn seemed to think it might be.'

'She's wrong.' And Summer would speak to her about it. 'I'm not anyone's responsibility.'

'You are when people care about you,' he said swiftly.

She snorted. 'People don't care about me. I'm not a priority—'

She stopped. 'I'm sorry,' she said. 'You didn't deserve that.'

'Except I think that I did,' he said softly. 'I'm sorry I made you feel that way.'

'I wasn't talking about you,' she said, raw.

'Doesn't mean it's not true.' He paused. 'I've spent my entire life knowing what it's like not to be a priority. I'm sorry I did the same thing to you.'

'You're not the only one.' She released a breath. 'I prioritised my own issues over our marriage.'

He nodded, acknowledging it. Then his face tightened. 'We don't have to talk about this. I just wanted to know that you're okay.'

'I am,' she said. 'I'm fine. So... I'll see you back at the party.'

She'd dismissed him—plainly and somewhat embarrassingly—and yet he didn't move. Instead, he kept his steady gaze on her, watching her. *Seeing* her. Just as he had the night at the Christmas party.

It broke something inside her, thinking that. She wished she could go back and start over. That they could start over. It was a futile fantasy. The only reason she was thinking it at all was because she was free of her father's secret with her family.

But she was still caught in it with Wyatt. She might think that he could get over her father's affair now, that it wouldn't affect what he was working towards, but it didn't change that she'd let it eat at their marriage. She'd let her feelings about being isolated in her family isolate her in her own marriage. Yes, Wyatt wasn't innocent in it, but neither was she. And it was time she took responsibility for it.

She'd broken the relationships in her life. She'd lost the man she'd loved—the man she still loved—because of it.

The realisation was too much for the pure will that had been holding back her tears. She felt her face crumple, heard her throaty sob, before she realised what was happening. She turned her back to him and pressed a fist to her forehead, embarrassed beyond measure that she was breaking down in front of him. That she felt safe enough to show him behind the mask now. *Now.* When she didn't know what he'd see.

Warm arms pulled her in before she knew he was even in front of her. His hand pressed gently against her head, encouraging her to lean against him.

She did.

Embarrassment fizzled as emotion took over, her mind once again handing the reins to her heart now that she felt secure. Her heart had no problem with breaking down from all the pain it had felt the last eight years. Pain that had started the moment she'd found out about her father's affair. Pain she'd stuffed down to the bottom of her heart. Pain that would no longer allow itself to be ignored.

She hadn't cried when she'd found out. Or after,

when her father had made his request. But she did now. She realised how much she'd lost now. How much her carrying that secret had cost her.

She'd thought she'd been protecting Wyatt by keeping the truth from him. She still believed that, though she recognised it as an excuse, too. Autumn was right, she had been afraid of getting hurt again. Not because she believed Wyatt would cheat on her. Not entirely.

She just didn't want to be left alone by the man who'd always managed to make her feel included. She didn't want to be cast aside, only to discover one day that her husband had replaced her with someone else. Most of all, she didn't want to lose being understood. Being seen. Especially after the years she hadn't been. She'd shut down when she'd thought that had happened. She'd thought it would be better if she chose it. But it wasn't. The defence mechanism had simply isolated her further.

She pulled away from him with that thought. She didn't deserve that he comfort her. She pressed her hand to her mouth, wishing she had a tissue so she could, at the very least, blow her nose. A handkerchief appeared in her line of vision. She mumbled a 'Thank you' before cleaning her face, and tried not to notice the make-up smudges on the white material.

When she looked up, his expression was kind.

'Don't look at me like that.' Her voice was strangled.

'Like what?'

'Like you feel sorry for me.'

'Not for you,' he disagreed. 'For what you're going through.'

'Well, don't,' she told him, straightening her shoulders. 'I deserve to feel this way. I put myself in this situation.' She paused. 'With some help from my father. But these were my actions, and—'

'Summer, I have no idea what you're talking about.'

She looked at him, and something inside her said, *Screw it*.

'I know. It's time that you do.'

Seeing Summer cry had shaken him. So had feeling her trembling body in his arms as the tears worked their way through her. Now she was staring at him with those big brown eyes wide, her mascara smudged, and her expression determined.

His stomach twisted at her beauty.

'Wyatt,' she said. He forced himself to focus on what she was saying. 'You're probably going to hate me after telling you this. I'm sorry.' She paused, bit her lip as tears gleamed in her eyes again.

Then she shook her head and swallowed.

'I'm sorry for what I've let it do to our relationship. And what it might do to how you see my father.'

'Your father? I don't—'

'He cheated on my mother,' she blurted out. Took a breath. 'Eight years ago, I found out before he told my mother and... He asked me to keep it a secret. From my mother and Autumn. Until the O'Brien deal went through, which was two months later.'

Her chest expanded and contracted. For some reason he found himself watching that instead of looking at her face.

'For two months, I watched my family be a family without me. I couldn't participate knowing what I knew. Even after they found out about the affair...' She took a breath. 'We didn't tell them I knew. It became this weight I carried with me. Like I was watching my family move on, move forward without me, and the weight kept me behind.'

It took a long time for him to reply, mostly because he hadn't realised she'd stopped talking. His brain had selectively taken in the information she'd told him. Now, it was playing it back so he could have all of the facts before he replied. It seemed like a safe way to do it. Yet when he spoke, he could have sworn he hadn't made any attempt at processing at all.

'Your father *cheated*?'

She gave a stiff nod.

'He asked you to keep it from your family?'

She nodded again.

'And from me?'

Her eyebrows rose, and she shook her head.

'Why didn't you tell me?'

'I—I didn't tell anyone.'

'I was your husband,' he said in a hard voice. 'I told you things I didn't tell anyone else.'

'Which made me realise I couldn't tell you!' she exclaimed. 'You were aiming for my father's life, Wyatt. It gave you purpose. A way out of what you went through with your parents.' She stopped to take a breath. 'How could I tell you that life didn't exist?'

'So your leaving wasn't because you thought you weren't what I wanted.'

She closed her eyes with a shake of her head. When she looked at him again, he felt the emotion there as if it were his own.

'It was a combination of the two. I knew I wouldn't be what you wanted because I knew that life didn't exist.'

'That's not the only reason you didn't tell me, though.'

'It's part of it.' Her eyelashes fluttered. 'The rest is… My father's secret isolated me from my family. Your determination to become him isolated me from—' She hesitated. 'From you.'

He saw that. Along with everything else he'd realised, he could see how she must have felt as though she'd had no choice but to leave. But it didn't keep him from getting angry that she hadn't told him the truth. That she'd made decisions for him. That she'd tried to protect him when, really, he'd needed her honesty.

'My father isn't someone you should look up to, Wyatt.'

'That isn't for you to say.'

Her head dipped. 'Do *you* say so?'

He took a moment to figure out the answer, then shook his head.

'I don't think I care.'

'You don't…' she repeated softly. 'This doesn't affect the way you see him at all? The way you see his life? The one you so desperately wanted to have?'

'No,' he said dismissively. When a tear trailed down her cheek, he clenched his jaw and tried to answer. 'It makes me see your father's human, like you tried to convince me last night.'

'You didn't believe me then.'

'I didn't know this.' He thought about it. 'In all honesty, it makes me like him even more. I don't like what he did,' he added quickly, when the colour disappeared from her face, 'but he made a mistake. Clearly he's made up for it or today wouldn't have happened.' He shrugged. 'He made a mistake and he still has a good life.'

'You respect him even though you know what he did? To my mother—to *me*?' Her voice was small.

He ran a hand through his hair. 'I don't know what you want me to say, Summer. He's been the most consistent presence in my life in the last nine years. Hell, he's been more consistent than my own parents were when they were still in the picture.' His hand dropped. 'This news... It's disappointing, sure, but it doesn't change our relationship.'

'But...'

She stopped, her face twisted in pain, and enough sympathy pooled inside him that he said, 'Summer.'

She didn't reply, just pushed that gorgeous mane of curls back and stared up into the sky. When she looked back at him, her eyes were steady.

'When you told me about your parents, I realised how significant your relationship with my father was. Is. I didn't want to be the one responsible for disillusioning you. Clearly I was wrong.'

'You were,' he said uncompromisingly.

'Because this doesn't change the way you think about my father?'

'No.'

She nodded, pursed her lips. 'Well, it did for me. I wasn't interested in repeating my mother's life. You were turning into my father,' she continued at his frown. 'What stopped me from turning into my mother? The woman who was second-best to my father's business? Who eventually slipped so far down on his list of priorities that he cheated?'

'You did,' he said after a moment. 'You stopped yourself from turning into her.'

'Damn right I did.'

'You thought you were protecting me, but you were really protecting yourself.'

'Clearly I needed to.'

He stared at her. 'I can't believe you'd say that.'

'I can't believe what my father did to me doesn't faze you in the least.'

'Because you did it to yourself.'

He saw her wince, but he refused to let it soften his heart.

'You chose to leave me instead of talk to me about this. You didn't even think about needing to protect me from *that*. From being abandoned one more time.' He barely paused to take a breath. 'I told you about my mother and father leaving and your first thought was about you.'

'I… No. I didn't want to hurt you.'

'No, you didn't want to hurt *yourself*,' he retorted. 'All because *you* couldn't face that your father was human.'

He was right.

The knowledge was worse than how coolly he'd responded to her father's affair. Or how he was focusing on the wrong thing in it all. No, not the wrong thing, she thought. The *right* thing.

She'd accused Wyatt of placing Trevor on a pedestal because that was what she had done. She'd told him to see her father as human because she hadn't. She hadn't allowed Trevor any space to make mistakes. To *be* human. She hadn't truly known him; only the version of him she'd created in her mind.

That version had been based on the man who had always been there, even if he'd been distracted. Who'd showed her such patience when teaching her about the Bishop business. Who believed in her enough to want her to take over. Who cared for her enough to show her how.

It hadn't considered the distractions when he was around. The focus on the business. She'd only seen her father's priorities after she'd discovered his affair. Realising that had opened her eyes to all of his weaknesses. And that had thrown her life into disarray.

Because she'd seen what she'd wanted to.

She'd done the same thing with Wyatt. Her actions in her marriage had been because she'd thought she knew how things would go. She'd projected so much of her father onto Wyatt she hadn't given him a chance to prove her wrong. She'd seen what she'd wanted to and acted according to that. His unexpected reaction now proved it.

She was wrong. Had been for so long.

How could she trust herself after that?

Her eyes fluttered to Wyatt's face, and she knew with certainty that, subconsciously, she hadn't trusted herself for the longest time. She'd fooled herself into believing she could because that was how Wyatt made her feel. He saw through the pretence and the hurt. Because of it, she saw through it, too. Enough that she'd agreed to marry him.

But that feeling hadn't stayed for long. When she'd realised what Wyatt had wanted, needed, she hadn't trusted herself to be able to give it. And her trust in herself, in her feelings for him, had diminished even more. So she'd used her father's affair to protect herself. She'd used her own response to it to anticipate what Wyatt's response might be, as if it were a test.

One she now knew she'd failed.

Her stomach churned. And though, logically, she knew it wasn't possible, her heart churned, too. It was so disappointed it couldn't trust its feelings for the man that filled it with warmth. The man it had never stopped loving. The man she'd never stop loving.

But that love didn't matter because it came from her. She couldn't trust that she hadn't fallen in love with someone who might hurt her. And she couldn't spend her life or their relationship trying to anticipate that hurt. Trying to protect herself from it. Trying to protect herself from *herself.*

She couldn't put Wyatt through that either.

'To think,' Wyatt said softly, oblivious to her inner turmoil, 'if you'd told me the truth, we might have still been married.'

She stared at him, and it was as if scales had fallen from her eyes.

'No,' she said. 'I don't think we would have been.'

'What?'

'You said you felt me pulling away from you. Which is true, I did. I didn't trust that I could give you what you needed from me.' She paused. 'But you pulled away from me, too, Wyatt.'

He frowned. 'I was…responding to you being distant.'

'I was responding to *you* being distant,' she shot back. 'You know that. But telling the story that way keeps you from being a hypocrite, doesn't it?' She didn't give him a chance to answer. 'You used your reaction to your parents' abandonment to anticipate my reaction, too. You thought I'd respond by telling you that you weren't what I wanted, so you pushed yourself harder to give me the life you thought I wanted.'

She shook her head.

'But that's not my point.'

'You have one?'

She ignored the jibe. 'If you felt me pulling away, why didn't you say anything?'

Confusion settled over his features. 'I thought… it was always going to happen, I guess.'

'But you tried to keep it from happening.' She paused. 'Why not just talk to me?'

'Are you punishing me?' he asked after a moment. 'Because I said you should have talked to me?'

'No,' she answered. 'I think you're right. I should

have spoken to you. If I could go back and change that, I would. But that doesn't mean we wouldn't have ended up here.'

He didn't reply. She sighed.

'Our relationship wouldn't have lasted, Wyatt. I can't be in a relationship. I don't trust myself. How can I expect to trust you?' She took a breath. 'But also because you don't want to be in the relationship. Not with me, not with anyone.'

CHAPTER SIXTEEN

'THAT'S NOT TRUE.' He shook his head vehemently. 'I asked you to marry me. Of course I wanted to be in a relationship. With you. How did this become about me anyway?' he asked. 'How are you blaming me?'

'We're both to blame for our relationship ending, Wyatt.'

He shook his head again.

'You just said you always thought I was going to leave,' she pointed out. 'How can you start a relationship expecting that?' And then she saw it. 'But you did. That's why you asked me out after knowing me for a few hours. That's why you asked me to marry you after knowing me for six months.' She almost laughed. 'You were setting our relationship up to fail.'

She waited for a reply. It didn't come.

'You didn't even fight when I asked for the divorce.'

'I asked you why,' he said mechanically.

'And accepted the obvious lie I told you.'

She removed the emotion from her voice, speaking coolly to try and combat the heat in his eyes. She had no intention of fighting with him. She was too tired. Tired of what the conversation had forced her to face. Tired of pretending: to herself, to the world. To Wyatt.

Pretending she didn't have feelings for him would likely be the death of her.

'Look, we should probably get back—'

'We're not done,' he interrupted.

'What more is there to say?' she asked, no longer keeping the fatigue from her voice.

'What about an apology?'

'I'm sorry.'

'What are you apologising for?'

'What do you want me to apologise for?'

'Summer—'

'No,' she cut him off. 'I'm done. We wouldn't have worked out. I don't know if I can trust who I think the people I love are and you're...' She lifted her eyes. 'You're far too afraid of someone leaving you to be fully invested in any relationship.'

'Why are you saying these things?' he asked. 'They're not true.'

She studied him, saw he believed what he was saying, and threw caution to the wind.

'Okay, then. Actually, it's perfect for me because I'm tired of the turmoil of keeping things to myself.' She paused for a second.

'I meant what I said on the beach last night. I... I love you. I love your work ethic and your loyalty. I love how freely you give of yourself to other people. *For* other people. I love how you see me.

How you've always been able to see me. I love this feeling—' she pressed a fist to the base of her stomach '—right here that heats and trembles whenever I'm near you.'

'*Summer.*'

His voice was breathless, his face stricken, and her mouth curved. She walked towards him, rested a hand on his chest, over his heart. Feeling the rapid beat of it, she exhaled shakily.

'Your heart's beating much too fast.' Her hand lowered to his stomach. 'And there's panic turning your stomach.' The hand lifted to his neck. 'Your throat's thickening, too.' She waited a beat. 'Am I right?'

He nodded.

'That's because you don't want me to be in love with you,' she whispered. 'You're terrified of being in a relationship.'

'This is not fair,' he rasped.

She studied him, then rose up on her toes and pressed the lightest of kisses to his lips. The feel of it sank right down to her toes.

'No, it's not,' she said gently. 'But it is what it is. We weren't meant to be, Wyatt. We won't ever be.'

With the pieces of her heart trailing behind her, she made her way back to the wedding.

After his conversation with Summer, Wyatt was tempted to let Trevor down.

He wanted nothing more than to go back to his

cabin, pack up his things, and return to Cape Town. In fact, he made it halfway to his cabin before sanity prevailed and he dragged himself back to the celebrations.

He couldn't disappoint Trevor, no matter how strong the temptation was. To him, that felt like proof Summer was wrong. He wasn't afraid of relationships. He'd had a long, stable one with Trevor for years.

His conscience had chosen that moment to remind him of the caution he'd exercised in that relationship. And how he'd panicked when Trevor had asked him to be in the ceremony. When Summer had told him her father saw him as family.

It might have been proof that he'd forged a relationship over the years, but it also proved that every step he'd taken had felt like a tremendous feat. A compelling argument in favour of Summer's words.

It had hooked into his brain, that thought—that realisation—so the reception was not a pleasant experience. He managed to avoid most of the chit-chat because of his conversation with Summer, but caught enough to be relieved when dinner was served.

He was seated at the same table as Summer and Autumn, though he'd been relegated to the opposite end of where they sat. Summer studiously avoided his gaze. When he made eye contact with Autumn, she mouthed the word 'sorry'. He nodded, though he wasn't sure what she was apologising for. The celebrations dragged out, though the formal part had been mercifully quick, so he had no reason to stay after the dessert was served.

When he was sure no one would notice his departure, he sneaked out of the venue and made it all of five metres before he heard his name. He waited when he turned and saw Autumn running towards him. He waited some more when she caught up with him, but not her breath.

'Running in sand is really *hard*,' she huffed, and his smile grew.

'Apparently.'

'Please, have some empathy.' She braced on her knees, then straightened. 'Not all of us are perfect human specimens.'

His eyebrows lifted. 'Was that meant to be a compliment?'

'It was a compliment, but it's kind of an insult, too, mainly because your tone suggested you were making fun of me. But it doesn't matter,' she said, waving her hand, placing both of her hands on her hips now. 'I'm not here to give you compliments.'

'How disappointing,' he said dryly.

She gave him a look. 'I wanted to say sorry about the tension during dinner.'

'It's not your fault.'

'I feel like it is,' Autumn admitted. 'I told her to tell you the truth… I encouraged you to go after her… I feel like I facilitated it somewhat.'

'Why?'

'I told you—'

'No, I mean why did you tell her to tell me the truth?' he interrupted.

'Oh.' She frowned. 'You guys still have feelings for one another.'

'I don't—' He broke off. 'I don't have feelings for her.'

Autumn's eyebrows lifted so high he was surprised they didn't disappear into her hair.

'Oh. I didn't realise we were ignoring the real world,' she commented. 'But her annoyance with you kind of makes sense now. She tells you she loves you, and—'

'She told you that?' he asked, his heart doing a strange skip in his chest. 'She told you she loves me?'

'Yes. Not that she had to,' Autumn said. 'She's never stopped loving you.' She made a face. 'Why are you pretending not to know this?'

'She said she loves me,' he replied slowly. 'She didn't say she's always loved me.'

Autumn snorted. 'Were your moves that good this weekend you thought you'd convinced her into falling in love with you again?'

He didn't know what to say.

She laughed, then her face sobered. 'Look, I know things are complicated. But the thing with my father, and the secret? It hurt her. We hurt her.' Autumn's face tightened. 'Despite that, she still told you she loved you. Tell me you don't think that means something.'

He couldn't.

Not that it mattered. He'd dealt with everything so poorly. Part of that had been because he'd wanted to tell her he loved her too.

He took a deep breath. 'You don't have to apologise,' he said to Autumn. 'None of this is your fault. Not really.'

She threaded her fingers together.

'I know I'm going to be out of line with this, but if you do have feelings for Summer—' her tone made it clear she believed he did '—you should prove it to her. Be there for her. Prove you are who she thinks you are.'

He nodded, but things were happening in his body again. The same things Summer had pointed out when she'd said she loved him. The pumping heart, the panicked stomach, the thickening throat. He ignored them and said goodnight to Autumn before making his way back to his cabin.

It was a peaceful walk, mainly because all the lodge's guests were still celebrating at the beach. It had taken him a while to realise no one other than the Bishop party was staying at the lodge for the weekend. But then, the Bishops were known for their wealth just as much as they were for their close-knit family. He supposed that was part of what upset him about Summer's secrets.

His entire career at Bishop Enterprises, he'd

idolised Trevor Bishop. Not only because of what the man had done for him, but because of what Trevor had achieved. He'd turned the company his father had started into one worth billions. All with a solid marriage and a happy family in tow.

Except hearing about Trevor's affair hadn't surprised him. Wyatt didn't care much for the moral implications of it, but he wasn't surprised. Which told Wyatt he'd suspected the life he'd idolised Trevor for couldn't be real. It proved he'd been after an illusion. An unattainable idea. Just as Summer had said.

Had he been so desperate for a better life than what he'd grown up with that he'd made up the one he was working towards? Or had he just allowed that illusion to obscure how much he wanted a family?

A little of both, he thought, though it was the last one that stung. It forced him to recognise what longing for a father-son, mother-son relationship meant. It forced him to face how much his parents had hurt him by leaving. How much Summer had hurt him by leaving.

Facing it made him realise how upset he was with himself. For creating the illusion. For believing it existed. He knew it didn't. But he'd needed to believe it did to get him out of the hole he'd been in during university.

He saw that now, clearly. Which meant he knew that part of why Summer had left had been valid. If she'd told him the truth, he would have been disillusioned sooner. Or he would have had to face the truth sooner. Would it have caused him to devolve into angry, aimless Wyatt? He didn't know. He supposed that uncertainty had prompted Summer into avoiding even the risk of it.

But if there'd been something inside him that had believed the idea didn't exist, shouldn't it have steered him away from relationships? It might not have been conscious, but considering his own relationship experiences, shouldn't he have run away from Summer?

You were setting our relationship up to fail.

Summer's words echoed in his head. They had that same heartbreaking quality to them as when she'd said them the first time. He'd been offended by the accusation then. He'd been angry and not thinking straight, and his instinct had been to lash out. But she was right. And so was he. There had been something that had steered him away from relationships. It hadn't been conscious, or mature, and so it had manifested itself in exactly the way Summer had said.

He *had* set their relationship up to fail.

He reached his cabin as that thought allowed a flood of emotions, of questions in. The last thing he wanted as that happened was to be confined between four walls. Before long, he found himself on the path leading down to the beach where he'd kissed Summer what felt like a lifetime ago.

It seemed right to be there. This was where things had changed between him and Summer. Or had that happened that night on the bridge, where he'd seen her vulnerable for the first time since she'd asked for a divorce? Where he'd allowed *himself* to be vulnerable for the first time since telling her about his parents?

Perhaps that was why he hadn't stopped feeling since that night. He'd opened the door and had forgotten to close it. Or had been unable to close it. Spending time with Summer seemed to have that effect. It scared him. Same as when he'd fallen in love with her all those years ago.

He'd gone into defence mode then. Or self-destruct mode. And he'd sabotaged his relationship with her. He'd proposed after six months of dating. He'd told her about his parents knowing it would change things for him. He'd spent their marriage pursuing a life he knew didn't exist. He'd let her down, countless times.

His heart ached at the way he'd treated her. Though he supposed there was something significant about that. He'd never felt the need to sabotage his relationships with other women in the same way. Not that he'd stuck around long enough to. His longest relationship before his marriage had been a year and he'd spent more than half that time travelling for work. He hadn't even considered feelings then. Now he saw he'd purposely orchestrated his life so he wouldn't have to.

Then Summer had come along. What he'd felt for her had been different. More intense. Scary. Instead of taking a step back and dealing with that fear, he'd identified all the exits and sped through the closest one when she'd presented it as an option. Hell, he hadn't only identified exits, he'd *built* them. Because of that fear.

That fear that had awoken in his veins when his father had left. That had taken residence when his mother had gone to rehab for the first time. That had dug in its roots and grown freely every time he'd had to go into foster care. That had overtaken everything when he'd come home that day and realised his mother had left for good.

He should have known the remnants of his past were still there. He should have seen his aversion to long-term relationships as a symptom of it. Should have seen his caution in his relationship with Trevor as a part of it. The fast pace of his relationship with Summer, too.

He should have realised he was protecting himself. Preparing himself. If he could protect himself—if he could prepare himself—maybe it wouldn't hurt so damn much when the people he cared about decided to leave.

Wyatt lowered to the sand, grabbed a fistful of it, and threw it into the receding waves as if somehow it would help him throw away his issues. Or the guilt that realising them brought.

He'd denied that he hadn't wanted a relationship with Summer. He stood by that. Because the truth wasn't that he didn't want it; he hadn't been ready for it. Everything that happened with Summer proved his feelings for her had been special. Considering that the fear was still throbbing heavily through his body, beating loudly in his ears, he thought those feelings might not only be in the past...

He looked around, saw the spot where he and Summer had lain in the sand. Where they'd shared things with one another. Where they'd opened up.

His eyes shifted to where he'd chased her on the sand. He could still hear her shriek of laughter. Could still feel the grin it had brought to his face.

And where he was standing had been where they'd kissed. Where he'd felt her soft body under his fingertips. Where the perfection of her lips had touched his.

There were other things racing through his mind, too. Like how Summer always put others above herself. Like how, despite how wealthy her family was, she hadn't sat back and enjoyed that wealth. How she'd gone out and made a name for herself. How she was the most down-to-earth person he knew.

She was the most caring person he knew, too. She loved deeply; hurt deeply. Having someone she cared about betray her trust must have stung. Feeling like an outcast because of it, though she'd done nothing wrong...

He could see how he'd made her feel isolated in their marriage. And how feeling that way with him must have hurt her.

He could also see why she'd want to protect him from that kind of hurt, too.

He stilled as warmth spread through his body at that. At how her thinking about wanting to protect him at all was more than either of his parents had done. She might have been misguided in her motivations for leaving him, but they were nobler than either of his parents', he was sure. And she'd done it all in spite of how he'd hurt her.

Besides, it wasn't a small thing that she wanted him to have the life he'd always wanted. She believed in him. Not in the way Trevor did, for his smarts or capabilities, but for who he was. For the person he was. Most of all, for who he had the potential to be.

It complicated things, these realisations. It complicated…feelings. He knew what those feelings were, but he didn't know what to do about them. Especially not when his fear still mingled with them. When he was still afraid of being abandoned.

When the sun started to light the sky, he wasn't any closer to knowing what he should do about them. Or the urgency accompanying them.

CHAPTER SEVENTEEN

SUMMER HAD PACKED her stuff before Autumn returned to the cabin after the wedding. When her sister walked in shortly after midnight, she greeted Autumn with her luggage.

'What's going on?'

'I'm leaving.'

Autumn's brows lifted. 'Right now?'

'I would have left much earlier if I hadn't waited to say goodbye to you.'

'Thank you for being so considerate,' Autumn replied dryly. 'Seriously, Sun, you can't leave now. It's after midnight.'

'You drove after midnight last night,' Summer reminded her.

'Because I needed to be here for Mom and Dad today. Not because I was feeling emotional and had to escape my ex.'

Summer's back went up. 'Really?' She narrowed her eyes. 'How is Hunter, by the way?'

Autumn's straightened. 'He's fine.'

'Hmm. Your friendship is going well, then, is it?'

Autumn folded her arms. 'Yes, actually it is.'

'So you wouldn't even be tempted into running

if you told him you loved him? And he didn't reply,' she added flatly, when Autumn opened her mouth.

There was a pause.

'Fine, I supposed I'd be tempted to.' Autumn threw her clutch onto the couch. 'But I wouldn't let him ruin the time I got to spend with my family because of it.'

'Of course you wouldn't, Autumn. You're perfect.'

Autumn tilted her head. 'Not sure I deserved that.'

Summer exhaled. 'No, you didn't.' She cleared her throat. 'But spending time with the family isn't exactly a pleasure for me.'

'I know,' Autumn said, her face softening. 'I'm sorry you went through that. I should have—'

'It's not your fault, Wind,' Summer interrupted, mostly because she didn't have the energy to dive into it. 'Look, I just need some space. And since there's little chance of me getting sleep tonight, I might as well make the best of the time.'

'Sun,' Autumn said slowly. Summer waited for the lecture. 'I don't want you to drive in this state. You didn't have any sleep last night either. At least try to get some rest. If you can't, I'll drive us home in the morning.' She put her hand on Summer's arm. 'Please, don't go.'

Summer studied her sister's face, saw the genuine concern there, and heaved out a breath. 'Fine. But first thing in the morning...'

Autumn crossed her heart, brought two fingers to her lips, and then lifted them to the air in the salute they'd created when they'd been kids.

Six hours later, Summer was kissing her sister on the forehead while Autumn slept, rolling her bags out the door.

She hadn't made the promise, she told herself when her conscience poked at her. Besides, she didn't want to cut short Autumn's time with their parents because of her emotions. She'd done that far too many times in the past. Things would change in the future. She'd make sure of it.

She packed her luggage into her boot. When she closed it, she jumped when her father appeared at her side.

'What are you *doing*?' she asked, pressing a hand to her heart.

'I saw you making your escape.'

'How?' Summer looked around. 'Your cabin is on the other side of the lodge.'

Trevor pursed his lips; Summer rolled her eyes.

'Autumn.' Summer frowned. 'She sent *you*?' She winced at the incredulity in her voice. Then, with a shake of her head, said, 'I'm sorry, I didn't mean that.'

'You did. It's fair.' Trevor gave her a steady look. 'How about we take a walk down to the beach before you go?'

Again? Summer wanted to ask, but caught the question before she could. Clearly Autumn thought she needed to speak with their father, which wasn't untrue. Summer had planned to have a conversation with him as part of her 'things would change' resolution. Although she hadn't counted on it being so soon.

When their feet touched the sand of the beach, Summer said, 'I have something to say to you,' at the same time her father said, 'I'd like to apologise.'

Then they both said, 'What?'

'Let me go first,' Trevor told her, 'since I need to say something I should have years ago.'

Summer nodded and put her hands into her jersey's pockets.

'I'm sorry, Summer. For the affair. For asking you to keep it a secret. For seeing what it did to you and not doing anything about it.'

Summer swallowed, shutting her eyes against the tears that immediately began to burn there.

'I should never have asked it from you. Or let you suffer for it as long as you did.'

She felt her father's hand on her wrist, and she stopped walking, opening her eyes. The sincerity on his face soothed her; the sadness unsettled her.

'I know I hurt you.' He cleared his throat. 'I thought it would be easier if I ignored—'

'Dad,' she interrupted. 'You don't have to explain. I know why you didn't do anything about it.'

'You do?'

'Yeah. It was easier to hurt me than to hurt Mom again. I get it.'

Trevor's face tightened. 'I'm so sorry, Summer.'

'I know.' She took a shaky breath and looked up. 'But I did some of it to myself, too.' She met his gaze. 'You hurt me. I felt…betrayed. About everything.' She started to look down, then forced herself to keep eye contact. 'I stopped trusting you because you weren't who I thought you were.'

Trevor's eyes gleamed, but the nod of his head was firm.

'I stopped trusting myself because of it. I thought you were one person, and you turned out to be another, and I didn't know how I missed it.' His eyes widened, but she kept talking. 'It's messed me up. I only saw how much this weekend.' She took a breath. 'I have a long way to go before I can put it behind me.'

Trevor looked down.

'But I'm willing to try.'

His head shot up. 'You are?'

Something similar to a smile touched her lips. 'Yeah. I'm taking responsibility for our family, too.' She waited a beat. 'So you can go back and tell Mom you apologised.'

His lips curved, but it wasn't a smile.

'I wanted to do this,' he said. 'I didn't do it because she told me to.'

She studied him, and saw a sincerity in his eyes that she hadn't for the longest time. She nodded, then stepped closer to him. Carefully, she wrapped her hands around his waist, rested her head against his chest. She felt his hesitation before his arms went around her, and they stood like that for a moment before stepping away.

She pretended not to notice the tears that trailed down her father's cheeks.

'I'm going to make it up to you,' Trevor promised.

She nodded, folded her arms. His eyes shifted to behind her.

'Starting now,' he said, moving forward and kissing her on the forehead. 'You should try with him, too, Sun.'

She frowned, opened her mouth to answer, but he was already walking away. When she turned, she saw Wyatt a few metres behind him.

Wyatt braced when he saw Summer's body tense, though he wasn't sure why. Would he chase her if she tried to run? Or would he have let her go, considering not five minutes ago he wasn't sure what he'd say to her when he saw her?

His heart immediately steeled with resolution, his mind following.

No more letting her go.

'You're up early,' she noted demurely.

'Not up early,' he told her. 'Going to bed late.'

An eyebrow quirked. 'You couldn't sleep?'

'Not after what happened last night, no.'

She studied him. 'Don't let me stop you.'

'Actually,' he said softly, 'I think I have to.'

'What?'

'You were here with your father,' he said, ignoring her question.

'Yes.'

'Everything okay?'

Her arms tightened at the front of her chest. 'It will be.'

'Good.'

A long pause followed his pathetic answer.

'Well,' she said, when the awkwardness reached peak level. 'I guess… I'm going to leave.'

'No, wait,' he said before she could, panic spurring the words. Then, when she didn't move, only looked at him expectantly, panic turned into fear. He'd never been more terrified in his life.

'Wyatt?'

'I built exits,' he said, 'in our relationship. I built…exits.'

'Am I supposed to know what that means?'

'Yes,' he replied. 'And you do.'

She bit her lip, then inclined her head in acknowledgement. 'You were looking for a way out.'

'I started our relationship knowing exactly where the ways out were. I… I helped create them. I pushed us both towards them with the way I behaved. So,' he added measuredly, 'you were right last night. We probably *would* have ended up here anyway.'

'You know,' she said after a few seconds, 'if you built the exits, I handed you the tools.' She paused.

'I was always afraid I wouldn't be able to trust you. Because I didn't—don't—trust myself. Or my belief of who you were. Because of what happened with my father. Or whatever,' she ended on a mutter, her face turning red.

Seconds ticked by.

'We were both wrong, then,' he said.

She lifted a shoulder. 'Or we were both right and this…didn't have a future.'

'Does it now?' he asked, through numb lips—and with a numb mind, since he had no idea where that question had come from.

Or no, wait, he did. It had come from the fact that she loved him. That he'd never stopped loving her. Suddenly it became clearer than it had ever been. That this was more important than the fear. That this was worth the chance.

'How can it?' she interrupted his thoughts. 'I still don't trust me. And you… You still don't want a relationship.'

A brand-new fear began to thrum through his body, more urgent than the other he'd let control his life. Finally he realised his past fears had been so extreme with Summer because he knew she'd be the most important person in his life. Which was why it had hurt so damn much that she'd given up on them.

Yet he'd given up on them, too.

But no more.

'What if I prove that you can trust you?'

She laughed softly. Heartbrokenly. 'How are you going to do that?'

'By showing you that you can trust who you think I am.' He reached for her hands. 'No matter how long that takes.'

Summer couldn't believe her ears. But there was warmth spreading through the icy coldness of her body; of her heart.

This is really happening.

Even in her worst nights after the divorce, when she'd missed him with everything inside her, she hadn't allowed herself to think about getting back together with him. Now that the possibility was here, she couldn't believe it.

'What if it never happens?' she asked.

It was easier to dread the worst than to hope for the best.

'Worst-case scenario?' he asked, brow furrowed. 'We spend our lives enjoying each other.'

'That's a big ask from someone who's spent his life running from commitment.'

'We prefer "fearing abandonment",' he said dryly, before his expression sobered. 'I know. So I suppose we won't only be proving you can trust me.' He paused. 'We'll be proving I'm… I'm safe with you.'

She studied him. Saw the passionate, resolute answers he'd give her if she asked him every question going through her mind on his face. In the light shining so fiercely in his eyes.

'That's a big ask from someone who doesn't love me,' she said quietly.

His eyes swept over her face. 'Are you fishing for compliments?'

'Why would I—?'

'Because you want me to tell you that I like you. Your dry humour and the way you put rich people in their place.' He plucked a stray curl and pulled it down, before letting the spiral bounce back up. 'I like how you get annoyed with me. With people. And with yourself. And your feelings.'

Her lips twitched, but he continued before she could say anything.

'I like how you care about me,' he said. 'That you tried to protect me, even if being honest with me would have been better.'

'Wyatt—'

'You should have been honest with me,' he interrupted, 'but I shouldn't have let you leave. I should have fought.' His lips curved, then straightened. 'I'm fighting now.'

Her eyes welled up with hope—that damn *hope* that wouldn't go away—but she shook her head. 'We haven't changed, Wyatt. I haven't changed—'

'That's not true,' he said, his fingers gently holding her chin. 'You've realised things about yourself. I've realised things about myself.' He paused.

'Are you telling me that hasn't changed you? Because it's certainly changed me.'

She thought about all the things she'd learnt after this experience. Like how she'd been too hard on her family. How maybe…maybe she'd been too hard on herself, too. And that she'd let both those things control her life for too long.

Which probably meant she had changed.

'You really want to try?' she asked huskily. 'You're not afraid any more?'

'I'm terrified,' he said with a raw laugh. 'But I'm more afraid of losing you.'

She blinked rapidly, but it did nothing to deter the tears that fell down her cheeks. 'I like you, too, for the record.' She cleared her throat. 'I like that you made something of yourself. I like how funny you are. I like that you see me. No,' she said, 'I *love* that you see me.'

She lifted a hand and cupped his cheek, then brought her lips up to his, kissing him with the rest of her answer. With the simple *I love you.* There was passion and romance and happiness in that kiss. When they parted, they were both breathing heavily.

'I love you, too,' he said with a breathless laugh. Her eyes filled again. 'Hey,' he said, 'hey, that's a good thing.'

'I know,' she said with a little sob. 'It's just that you knew exactly what I was saying with that kiss and I haven't slept properly in weeks and I'm so tired.'

He laughed and pulled her into his arms. 'I know, baby.' He kissed her head. 'How about we get some breakfast and then some sleep?' He paused. 'Then make our way down to reception to extend our stay here.'

She pulled back. 'Why?'

'I don't know.' Colour curled up his neck, and Summer hid her smile. 'I thought it might be nice to stay here and get to know one another again. It's an idea. A terrible one, it seems, but...' He trailed off. 'Why are you looking at me like that?'

'I'm waiting for you to tire yourself out,' she said with a smile. 'I like the idea, Montgomery. It would be kind of nice to have a little holiday at the beach. If you promise to keep the water to yourself. I'm not having you "accidentally" throw it on my back while I'm suntanning again.'

He grinned. 'No promises.'

'Mont—'

He silenced her with a kiss. And for the first time in for ever, Summer felt like the sun.

EPILOGUE

'FIVE YEARS LATER, and still as beautiful as ever.'

'Why, thank you,' Summer said lazily, not bothering to open her eyes. 'Anything is possible with a balanced diet and exercise regime.'

'You know I wasn't talking about you.'

'And yet I answered, Montgomery,' she replied, opening her eyes and pushing herself up on the beach towel she was suntanning on. 'Probably because I'm tired of you saying how beautiful this place is. We've been here for three days. It's time to get over it.'

'Don't sound so bitter,' he told her with a grin. She used the moment to enjoy him standing shirtless in front of her. 'This is our special place.'

Before she could respond, he was scooping her into his arms.

'I'm not bitter,' she continued as if he hadn't picked her up. 'I just don't want you to turn into that person who repeats the same things. By the way, what are you doing?' she asked calmly.

'What I should have done five years ago.'

'To clarify—that would be to drop me into the ocean?'

'Correct.'

Accepting her fate with a nod, Summer threaded her fingers behind Wyatt's neck. She couldn't even muster up annoyance that Wyatt was threatening to throw her into the ocean. Again. Every time they got near a body of water, Wyatt went through the same routine. Not once had he thrown her in.

Though this was different, Summer knew. For the first time in five years they'd returned to the lodge where they'd rekindled their relationship. Where Wyatt had threatened to throw her into the ocean that very first time. It was enough to make her nostalgic.

It wasn't an emotion she felt regularly; her present was much better than her past. Though she did have a fondness for the last time they'd been on this beach together. They'd recommitted to their relationship. And every day in the last five years, they'd grown stronger.

They hadn't rushed into their relationship this time. There had been no jumping past important steps. No spontaneous engagements. She and Wyatt had taken the time to build something beautiful. And they'd succeeded.

The first thing Wyatt had done when they'd got back to Cape Town was hire an assistant. It had helped him with the pressure at work, which left most of his evenings free. He and Summer spent their free time together as far as was possible, and

Summer had no doubt Wyatt had prioritised her. She made sure she did the same for him.

The slogan for their rekindled relationship was that work was important, but the other was more important. Cheesy, but it worked.

The time they'd spent together had allowed them a safe space to work through their issues. Summer had learnt to explore her trust issues; Wyatt, his fears. Acknowledging that they had issues had been an incredible step forward. As had being honest with each other. There was communication and laughter. Disagreement and arguments. Make-up kisses and…more.

They'd forged a different relationship with her family, too. Wyatt had become more realistic in his expectations, which had allowed him to bond with her family. And Summer had allowed herself to be…herself. To be *freely* herself. There were weekly family dinners; business consultations with the previous and current CEOs of Bishop Enterprises; spa dates and event planning with her mother and sister.

So much had changed in the last five years. Summer couldn't imagine her life getting any better.

The thought stilled something inside her and Summer leaned back, content in Wyatt's arms.

'You aren't concerned about this at all, are you?' Wyatt asked, glancing down.

'Nope,' she said brightly.

'That takes some of the fun out of it.'

'Why do you think I'm approaching it this way?'

'Calling my bluff?'

'Even if you throw me into this water, my love, I will forgive—'

The rest of her sentence was engulfed by the water. She could still feel Wyatt's arms around her, which then dragged her up before she could fully process what had happened.

'What were you saying?' he asked with a grin, wiping the water from his face.

'Nothing,' she said through clenched teeth. She pushed her hair out of her own face. 'Though I'll admit, I didn't think you'd do it.'

'But you forgive me.'

She grunted, and he laughed before picking her up again. He stopped and set her down where the waves could only reach their feet.

'If it makes you feel any better, I did it for a reason.'

'Yeah, I know,' she said, folding her arms over her chest when a blast of wind made her shiver. 'You were being a jerk.'

'No.' His voice had thinned. Almost as if he were nervous. 'I didn't want you to expect this.'

'I didn't expect it,' she said dryly. 'I thought you were—'

That was when she saw him kneeling on the ground.

It took her a long time to find her voice.

'Well,' she said, barely louder than a whisper. 'You're right. I didn't expect this at all.'

Now the nerves danced across his face.

'In a good way or bad way?'

'Which way do you want it to be?' She laughed at his expression. 'A good way. Of course a good way. As if you didn't know,' she scoffed lightly.

He nodded—still nervous, which made her smile—before taking a box out of his pocket.

Y'You've wet it,' she said before she could help herself.

'It's sealed.'

He opened the box, took a small plastic bag out and reached inside it to reveal the most beautiful diamond ring. It was nothing like the one he'd first got her. That one had been large and ostentatious; part of what he'd thought she'd wanted, he'd told her later. This ring was a simple solitaire design.

It was perfect.

'So,' she said after a moment. 'Are you going to ask me?'

'I'm trying to figure out whether you want me to.'

'The past five years that I've stuck around haven't been enough to convince you?' she asked gently.

'No, they have,' he said, his teasing expression sobering. 'They absolutely have.' He took a shaky breath. 'I've felt safe with you for every day of these last five years. Every time my mind would expect you to leave. If we had an argument, or a disagreement. Or things went from easy to hard. But you didn't.' His eyes shone. 'And my heart told my mind it was a fool for thinking it.'

Another breath.

'I waited much too long to ask you this, especially considering I bought the ring a month into our new relationship.' He smiled. 'Will you marry me, Summer Bishop?'

Summer took the ring, slid it onto her hand.

'Does that give you your answer?'

He laughed and stood, pulling her in for a kiss. She put every single thing inside her in that kiss. When he leaned back, his eyes told her he knew all the things she wanted to say to him. There was time to say them all out loud later.

'Yes,' she said, reaching down and taking the plastic bag and ring box from him. 'In case you need to hear it.'

'I do.'

'I know.'

She took the ring off, put it back into the bag. Then she put the bag in the ring box and slipped the box into his pocket.

'What are you doing?'

'It's called payback, darling.'

'Pay—'

She didn't hear the rest. She was too busy tackling him into the ocean.

* * * * *

Look out for the next story in the
Billionaires for Heiresses duet

From Heiress to Mom

Coming soon!

If you enjoyed this story,
check out these other great reads
from Therese Beharrie

Her Festive Flirtation
Surprise Baby, Second Chance
Tempted by the Billionaire Next Door

All available now!